FOR LOVE'S SAKE ONLY

Helen and Hugh Kendall's pottery business is doing badly. So is their marriage — Hugh is having an affair with the new designer, Maureen Bradley. Under the pressure, Helen moves out and falls ill. Oblivious to this, Hugh goes with Maureen to Australia, ostensibly on a business trip. Helen plumbs new depths of depression until her flagging ego is restored by businessman Geoff Rowland. An enlightened Hugh returns from Australia to find Helen in hospital. But can things ever be the same again?

Books by Judy Chard
in the Linford Romance Library:

SEVEN LONELY YEARS
HAUNTED BY THE PAST
OUT OF THE SHADOWS
WHEN THE JOURNEY'S OVER

JUDY CHARD

FOR LOVE'S SAKE ONLY

Complete and Unabridged

LINFORD
Leicester

First published in Great Britain in 1988

First Linford Edition
published 2006

British Library CIP Data

Chard, Judy
    For love's sake only.—Large print ed.—
Linford romance library
1. Love stories
2. Large type books
I. Title
823.9′14 [F]

ISBN 1–84617–448–1

Published by
F. A. Thorpe (Publishing)
Anstey, Leicestershire

Set by Words & Graphics Ltd.
Anstey, Leicestershire
Printed and bound in Great Britain by
T. J. International Ltd., Padstow, Cornwall

This book is printed on acid-free paper

1

Helen Kendall gazed round the tiny country church she knew so well. Now it was filled with the perfume of summer flowers. The choir were singing 'Morning Has Broken', which Julie had chosen to be used while she and Brough signed the register.

Things were very different from the day when she had married, Helen mused. Then it had been traditional wedding hymns — 'O Perfect Love' and the Mendelssohn music . . . now it was either this tune, or 'Amazing Grace' and Vivaldi. Nostalgia washed over her, the words of the service brought back such memories of her own wedding day — she had stood beside Hugh, tall, handsome, attentive, and promised to love, honour and obey . . . It had been the fashion then, at least she had been old fashioned enough to want the word 'obey' left in. She was 20 and Hugh 22 . . . twenty years ago, two decades. A little sigh escaped her. So much had happened, so much had changed. Then she had been not long out of college with a degree in Art, the world her oyster. Her designs had won praise from many people outside the college as well as within its walls. She had been compared with such people as Willi Soukop and even David Leach. She had fallen under the spell of the pottery side of Art, partly perhaps because in a changing uncertain world where tastes and fashions altered like the direction of the wind, it was something which had continued for thousands of years: a method, material and produce which basically never changes, although the design itself might.

She soon discovered that making pottery for a living is hard work, hard physical work, an exhausting strain if the potter is determined to maintain and improve high artistic standards as she was. There were very few rich potters — but Hugh had been full of ideas and plans.

'I've got some good contacts in the commercial world, although I haven't been in it all that long,' he had grinned at her, 'you'll be the producer and I'll get the orders rolling in.'

In spite of some misgiving that it was a precarious way to make a living, she had believed him. Tentatively she said, 'Wouldn't it be better if you kept your job on just for a while, let us get on our feet, treat the pottery as a side line?'

He brushed her protests aside, 'You have to take a chance in life sometimes, Helen. Who was it that said 'There is a tide in the affairs of men, Which, taken at the flood, leads on to fortune . . . '?'

She nodded, 'Inevitably Shakespeare in *Julius Ceasar*, and I have to admit the end of the quote says 'Omitted all the voyage of their life Is bound in shallows and in miseries.''

'There you are then,' he hugged her 'a chap like that couldn't be wrong!'

She adored him and was prepared to

believe anything he said, never mind Shakespeare. There was only one small cloud on her horizon, she wanted a family as well as a career, but it had been two years before Gail was born. Even then she had had to persuade Hugh into the idea.

He looked sulky, 'We've got each other, love, kids can spoil a marriage whatever people like to say. Not only that, it'll sap your energy, divide your loyalties, bound to . . . dull your creativity even.'

But for once she had been adamant. 'It'll probably increase it,' she said firmly, 'after all having a baby is quite a creative process!' She had kept her tone light, trying to cajole him, but he had not been amused.

As if fate had not been on her side, she had a difficult pregnancy. During the last months she had to drag herself to the drawing board, but the little grim lines round Hugh's mouth had goaded her on. She had to show him, please him. In those days it hadn't been the fashion for husbands to be present at the birth of their child. In some ways she was glad. She had a bad time and found herself calling out his name in pain and fear. Although she didn't think for a moment he would actually have said 'I told you so!', in some ways he had been right, and the doctor had said no more babies. She knew Hugh had been relieved, she hoped because of her health and welfare, but a niggling little doubt suggested it might be because of her work . . . So Gail was a precious only one. A beautiful, happy child.

Hugh was ambitious, a real livewire, he had every kind of idea for expanding the business, even coffee parties on the lines of the Tupperware scene, when some of her best pieces were unobtrusively but well displayed. She found people asked her to make things to order. Hugh carefully checked retail prices in the shops and charged a little under without being too low, so they could raise them later.

'The great thing is to specialise,' he

said 'some people ask for a tea set with a larger teapot than usual, with a dinner set they want two gravy boats, for some reason best known to themselves, or a larger meat dish if they have a big family, so ours is not to reason why, give them what they want.'

Soon they didn't need to give the parties. They travelled round the Craft fairs all over the West Country, from their home just outside Tormouth. They shared a stall with a jewellery maker, but soon they were well known enough to afford their own. The weeks before Easter and Christmas were hectic — and lucrative. Gail went everywhere with them in her carrycot, always happy and smiling, taking no objection to being put in the back of the beat-up van they used. Eventually they had stalls in several markets, which meant keeping up a big stock of pottery. The Sunday markets were the best, so they worked a seven day week. There were times when Helen would have given anything just to lie in bed and sleep till lunch time, or sit in the tiny pocket-handkerchief garden outside their cottage on the edge of town, but always Hugh spurred her on.

'We're going to make it to the top, love, have our own pottery factory, employ people, just you see. Then you'll be able to rest.'

But somehow they never seemed quite to achieve this and because she loved him, she drove herself.

Hugh had built up quite a reputation now in all the shops which sold crafts in the county and down into Cornwall. He had bought a second small van so he could carry samples while Helen used the other for picking up materials, plastic bags of clay and so on.

They had even had their own exhibition in the village hall just up the road from the church where she sat now, waiting for Julie and Brough . . .

Julie had been one of the really good things that had happened to them . . . the time had come when they had had to take on another designer to help

Helen. Julie had come from Art College, the same one at which Helen had studied. That was 12 years ago . . . then she had met Brough who came from Australia and he had swept her off her feet . . .

As she came down the aisle now, radiant, she gave Helen a conspiratorial wink as she passed the end of the pew where she sat. Helen remembered how she had said 'Thought I was on the shelf for keeps,' and Helen had replied with a touch of sadness, 'It'll be like losing a daughter, love.'

Now in a cloud of Yves St Laurent perfume, she reached the church door on Brough's arm, looking so young in the cream Laura Ashley dress, with a straw hat, summer flowers twined around the brim.

The church emptied quickly as everyone sped off to the reception at the local pub. The place was packed to the rafters with friends and well wishers; Julie was very popular, as was Helen. People were a little more wary of

Hugh, he could have a sharp tongue, and one or two of the local husbands had been a bit suspicious of his good looks and charm. But all that was forgotten now as the champagne flowed and the hubbub became more and more deafening.

Julie had opted for a buffet rather than a sit down meal, 'Trouble is you get landed next to some crashing bore and you're stuck so you can't enjoy yourself. It's much better to be able to circulate even if it means balancing a plate in one hand and your glass and handbag juggling in the other!'

She was surrounded by a chattering, laughing crowd of young people. She had cast aside her hat in typical Julie fashion and was waving her glass about as she made some point, regardless of the golden liquid sloshing dangerously near the brim.

'My dear, it wasn't any good me having a floaty, romantic dress,' Helen heard her explaining to someone, 'Dear old Brough has a sheep farm as you know and it's hardly the done thing for 'sheilas' to swan about in anything but jeans and tee shirts, floating chiffon isn't really on.' She took a deep gulp of champagne, 'Still, that suits me, you know what I'm like!'

When Hugh had heard that Julie was going to Australia he had said quickly, 'Keep in touch, kiddo. There could be room for an up-market operation like Kendalls in Aussieland . . . always willing to consider emigrating.'

At that moment Julie caught sight of Helen standing alone, the tide of people had ebbed away for the time being. Quickly disengaging herself, she came over.

'Hi, boss!' She had always called Helen boss as a joke. Their relationship was hardly one of boss and employee . . . there was far more to it than that. 'What a hassle, hope you're getting your quota of champers. I never seem to have an empty glass. Jolly good job I'm not driving.' Helen grinned back. Julie was one of the most infectious people, mood-wise, that she knew.

'I've had my quota, don't worry.' Suddenly she couldn't help it, she said, 'It's going to be odd without you. I don't think it's really come home to me properly yet.'

Julie put her arm round her, once again with great threat to her glass. 'We had some good times, some funny ones too. Remember that rather odd dogsbody we had, what was his name? Joe, that's it. He always reminded me of Benny in Crossroads, never saw him without that incredible hat he wore. I'm sure he went to bed in it . . . anyway that's beside the point, he forgot to switch the regulator on the new kiln, and everything was baked to a biscuit . . . we'd sat up all night making the stuff . . . '

Helen giggled. 'Yes, I'll never forget that. I didn't know whether to laugh or cry. His face was a picture when he realised what he'd done.'

'Off the record, he used to call you Metal Mickey,' Julie went on, 'He said you had eyes in the back of your head and were everywhere at once like some super Dalek or robot.'

'God knows it was necessary,' Helen said, looking away for a moment, 'I tried to be everywhere at once and simply stopped being creative. I realise that now.'

'That's something that can never happen,' Julie said quickly.

'Well, one thing's for certain, we'll never be able to replace you in many ways, not just work. Imagine anyone else thinking up those wind bells . . . they were quite brilliant.'

Julie giggled again, her cheeks were pink, her eyes bright and shining. Helen thought she had never looked so pretty.

'I wonder if I looked like that on my wedding day,' she thought with a pang of remorse.

'Don't remind me of those bells,' Julie was saying, 'Gosh we had our problems there, what with the terrific heat they needed to be fired, and not knowing what to use for colour because of it. None of the usual paints or enamels would stick, remember?'

'Dark tan boot polish was a stroke of genius, and no one guessed!'

'Happy days!' Julie sipped her champagne. 'Thank goodness we're not flying until tomorrow morning and we've got a taxi laid on. I feel quite squiffy . . . it's not very romantic, the hotel at Heathrow, but convenient . . .'
Helen felt near to tears once more at the mention of Julie's imminent departure. She kissed her quickly,

'Must be the champagne has got to me, and the thought of you leaving.'

Julie put her arm round her. 'No one is indispensable, and anyway your ideas were always much better than mine. We were a good team. You'll find someone with a fresh outlook . . . it'll be good for the firm. It's easy to get stale, in a rut.'

At that moment Hugh came over to see what they had their heads together about. 'Sounds like yours truly talking, that last remark, Jules . . . you're too right kiddo, but I don't know how I'm ever going to persuade that wife of mine along those lines . . . you have to speculate to accumulate someone once said, I can't get that into her head.'

Although his tone was light, his eyes were hard as he looked at Helen. She felt a wave of resentment. It was all very well for him, going out and about, talking to, meeting people . . . she had to try to assess the mood of the people and yet keep the very high standard Kendalls had . . .

'We need to think along the lines of mass production, we have to face up to the fact that sales are dropping off. The public want something more up market, more with it.' Hugh was in full flow now on his favourite hobby horse. 'I was thinking the other day about that painting you used to see hanging in everyone's sitting room, in the pubs and cafes, the madonna type lady with the green face, remember?'

Julie burst out laughing, 'No I don't and you have to be joking . . . it sounds quite sick. Not our line, Hugh. We've always been original, a bit exclusive.'

'Exactly,' Helen said shortly, 'we've had a good reputation, the kind of reputation people like Wedgwood have built up for quality and exclusiveness.'

Now it was Hugh's turn to laugh. He threw back his head and guffawed. It was not a particularly kindly sound.

'My dear sweet Helen, you have to be joking now. You can hardly compare the small sparrow of Kendalls with the giant eagle of Wedgwood.'

Julie joined in the laughter, but hers was softened by the words, 'Oh I don't know; personally I think Helen has had some of the most brilliant ideas that Josh might have given his back teeth for . . . how about those clay birds — ocarians which you played like a flute? Or the cartoon characters, Syd and Goofy were just hilarious — magic.'

Hugh raised his brows and gave her a gentle pat.

'Anything you say, my queen. It is your day, bless you.' He bent and kissed her. Helen noticed the girl turned her head quickly so the kiss landed on her cheek and not her lips.

Someone came now and claimed the bride . . . Hugh wandered off to look for more champagne. The hubbub seemed louder than ever as everyone got a little drunk. For a moment Helen thought she would faint from the heat and noise. She found it difficult to get her breath. She made a bee-line for the powder room, somewhat grandly named by the landlord, although it was spotlessly clean but rather modest for such a grand title.

She sank on the one and only chair, undoing the jacket of her suit, wiping the perspiration from her face. Once or twice lately she had had this feeling of having to gasp for breath, particularly when she was a bit het-up or worried. She had put it down to her age. She supposed she was approaching the menopause. It affected different women in many ways she knew. Some sailed through it without a backward glance, some did not, in fact one of the women in the village who had always seemed to be so vigorous and healthy, into everything, had become mentally deranged and her husband had had to give up his job to look after her.

Panic rose within her . . . suppose it affected her in that way. What would Hugh do? Certainly not give up anything, she thought with a touch of bitterness. Quickly she shrugged off the idea. She was overweight . . . she must take some exercise, even perhaps join Gail at her aerobic classes in the holidays. She wasn't sure what they were, but her daughter seemed to enjoy them, apart from the stiffness the day after. She had said once, 'There are people there the same age as you, Mum. It only means you take things a bit more slowly. The teacher is really good.' She heard footsteps approaching, two women were coming towards her, laughing and chattering. Quickly she got to her feet and bent over the basin, splashing her face with the cool water.

2

The cottage felt strangely empty without Julie. She had lived with them since joining Kendalls and become like one of the family. Gail was away at college, and had returned there on the evening of the wedding. For the first time for years Helen and Hugh were alone. It was an odd feeling. They were almost like strangers. Always there had been the three of them, eating together, chatting over coffee after supper, talking of new designs, things that had happened in the factory, customers . . . Julie had often helped her in the tiny garden where she had grown herbs and sweet smelling old fashioned flowers for the pomanders she made. She had used some of the blossoms as models for the beautiful delicate flower shapes she had created.

'Do you know Julie, those carnations

are so life-like I can almost smell them,'
Hugh had said, and that had been quite
something for him, usually he wasn't
particularly observant of the artistic
side of the business. 'It's the brass, lass!'
he'd say in a pseudo Yorkshire accent,
'that's what counts.'

Julie had protested, 'It's the designs
we make that bring in the brass!' But it
had all been gentle banter, nothing
sharp or acid about it, somehow she felt
that lovely atmosphere had gone,
vanished with Julie.

Hugh brought home the account
books. He laid them on the table when
they had finished their silent meal.

'You'd better come and see the truth
for yourself in black and white, Helen.'
He paused a moment, 'Perhaps it would
be more accurate if I said red and
white. We really have the most horren-
dous overdraft. God knows how we'll
survive till Christmas.'

Helen looked at him in amazement.
She knew things had been a bit dicey,
but not that serious. 'I thought since

we'd moved and the workshops had been enlarged, the electric kilns installed . . . '

'That's all very pretty,' he broke in impatiently, 'but all that air drying lark, the modelling clays, they were expensive, and as the process is so damned slow, orders get delayed, people won't wait. Competition is needle sharp.'

'Surely the shop at least is doing well. It always seems to be crowded.'

'Mostly with lookers, not buyers. It's been a lousy season. The wet summer meant lots of people cancelled their holidays and flew to Spain on impulse and a cheap flight.'

'Why on earth didn't you say something before?'

He shrugged, 'What was the good? Half the time you don't listen to anything I say.'

'That's not fair!' She was near to tears, she could feel the breathlessness coming on again. She had worked so hard, been happy; she realised that almost imperceptibly things had changed. Perhaps it was from the time Julie got engaged and they knew they would have to look for a new designer. No, she couldn't put all the blame on that. But she did wish Julie had chosen to live in England and stayed on with Kendalls. No, the change had been between herself and Hugh, a subtle change, something had gone wrong since that day she had stood in the slanting sunshine in the little village church and plighted her troth. Perhaps she hadn't realised how ambitious Hugh was, eager to expand almost to the point of being ruthless. Was this sense of failure a threat to his manhood in his eyes? That precious macho image which seemed so important to a man of his age.

His voice was running on. 'We shall have to cut down on staff, last in first out. That new couple you took on last month, Kathie something and Frank Taylor, quality inspectors. They're a bit slow, some of their work is inclined to be sloppy, they have let one or two imperfections through, can't risk complaints.'

'Well they're young. We have to give

them a chance. After all both Julie and I made mistakes, lots of mistakes while we gained experience. Everyone has to learn.'

'Youth is no excuse and they can learn at someone else's expense, not mine.' He said shortly, gathering up the books. 'I've got an appointment with Baker, the bank manager, on Friday, see if he has any suggestion to make. They seem to give bits of kids overdrafts at the drop of a hat, maybe we could take out a second mortgage on the cottage.'

Helen looked at him with horror. 'But it's the one stable thing left ... paid for ... our own ... ' At first she didn't realise the implication of what she had said — 'The one stable thing ... ' but the expression on her husband's face told her plainly he had. He went out slamming the door behind him and drove off in the car with a crunch of gravel.

Next morning she went to the factory early. Hugh had left an hour before for

London to try and whip up some business. In spite of the fact that he had told her to sack Kathie and Frank — a job which she contemplated with dread — he still agreed they needed another designer. The design work and basic production planning, with all the other problems of factory management were too much for Helen to manage on her own, and he had now to be away more and more. She felt desperately tired. An odd tiredness, not entirely physical, as if her very brain were weary.

She had put an advertisement in the trade papers and the local Job Centre before Julie had left. There was a pile of replies on her desk. She hadn't had the heart to tackle them before, but now she must. Unemployment at 15% in the area meant any likely opening was pounced on whether the applicant was really suitable or not. Hugh had said airily,

'It'll be simple to find a new designer. They're ten a penny, the colleges, techs and polys are turning them out like sausages these days, all with Art degrees and high qualifications.'

'But that isn't what we want,' she protested, 'we need someone very special, someone like Julie, not that we'll ever be able to replace her.'

He had retorted impatiently, 'Don't be such a sad sack. Jules was good I grant you, but she wasn't unique and no one is indispensable.' Helen remembered that Julie had used that very expression herself.

'To me she is . . . ' she murmured.

Now she went through the letters. Some were so badly written and spelt she could hardly decipher them. Most of them had all the necessary diplomas or degrees, some were almost begging to be given the job, some were frankly arrogant as if the world owed them a living. The fact that they had been to university should guarantee they knew all about running a pottery business or any other, about design and the market requirements. Helen picked out a dozen which looked the most hopeful and asked them to come for an interview.

It was the end of the week before Hugh returned. She could tell he had had a bad trip. She knew him so well that his slightest mood communicated itself to her. Now he was aggressively cheerful, cracking stupid jokes, suggesting they go out for a meal. He smelt strongly of whisky.

'Honestly, I'd rather not. I've made a pie and feel too tired to dress up.'

He rounded on her impatiently, 'You're always too tired these days! Too tired to design anything decent, too tired to go out, even too tired in bed.' He turned on his heel. She heard him go out once more and start the car. She dropped her head on her hands as the tears coursed down her cheeks. He would have gone to the pub. It would be after midnight when he returned. Apart from anything else, she was terrified he would lose his driving licence and they would have to hire a driver to take him on his sales rounds, more expense. With a little stab of guilt she realised his personal safety hadn't been her prime consideration . . . had her feelings really come to that?

On Monday she interviewed twelve of the applicants and short listed six. Apart from their ability to design, it was going to be important that they fitted in as people whom she could work beside, for this was very necessary in the kind of creative work they would be engaged upon.

She was bone tired by the time she reached the tenth — Maureen Bradley. She really wasn't quite sure why she had short listed this one. She had no academic qualifications, and yet there had been something about her letter which appealed to her. It had been neither over confident nor arrogant, and yet she had set out what Helen assumed to be a true, unvarnished picture of the actual experience she had had, which was wide. She had worked in ceramics in Italy and Spain, and her hand writing was quite beautiful.

She had knocked and entered with a

certain amount of self assurance when Helen called 'Come in.' She had given her age as twenty-five but she looked less in some ways. She was tall and strikingly good looking. At first glance she did not seem beautiful, but the more Helen looked at her face the more she became aware of something deeper than beauty.

'Please sit down.' She realised the girl was waiting for her to speak, she sat with consummate grace as if she were a trained model. Her face was a pale oval, she had long, straight, glossy hair. She reminded Helen of a cross between an Italian painting of the Madonna, and the *Mona Lisa*. There was something elusive about her, enigmatic perhaps. She was polite but reserved.

She had brought a portfolio of designs with her. They were in complete contrast to most of the others Helen had seen, which had been conventional, stereotyped, unimaginative. As far as her work was concerned the girl had a self assurance, a confidence, knowing they were good, different, original.

Why don't I like her? Helen asked herself. It's unfair. I've only just met her. She couldn't be more pleasant. Heaven forbid I am jealous; she knew the designs were way beyond anything she could have conceived, out of her league, even better than Julie's work but somehow she seemed the kind of person one would never know, as if some impenetrable invisible shell covered her.

She answered all Helen's questions clearly and frankly, her wide blue eyes candid and childlike.

'Yes, I did go to Art School, but they didn't like my style and I didn't much like their methods, so we parted company.' The shadow of a smile played round her full lips. Somehow Helen got the impression she had been right and the college wrong.

'I had a portfolio of designs and a firm in Italy were advertising for an assistant designer. I flew out on spec and got the job. I think really it was my sense of colour they liked. Then I moved on to Spain. Of course ceramics there are often primitive in design, but again their sense of colour and design is beautiful. Even the street signs are individually created in ceramics.'

'May I ask why you left?'

The girl looked away. It was the first time Helen felt she had been a little thrown by the questioning. 'There was a little trouble, personal trouble, nothing to do with my work I assure you.'

'I see.' Helen wasn't quite sure if she could. This girl was essentially a private person, perhaps there had been a love affair, illicit maybe. Whatever it was she felt the leaving had been Maureen's decision. Julie had been such an extrovert, it was no good comparing them.

'I have several more people to interview. I'll be in touch. Thank you for coming.'

The girl got up slowly, uncurling like a cat, 'Perhaps you would be kind enough to let me know one way or the other fairly soon. I too have other interviews.' It could have been rude, but the way she said it made it seem a perfectly reasonable request.

'Of course,' Helen said quietly.

Hugh saw the letters and designs and her comments. He interviewed the short list of six. It included Maureen.

He came into her office. 'This is the one.' He held out Maureen's letter. Intuitively Helen had known she would be his choice.

'She hasn't any qualifications. She was only at college for a year and I think possibly left under a bit of a cloud. She's been free-lancing more or less since, except for a couple of jobs abroad.'

'I don't care if she left college under a load of hay, she is out of the ruck, and that is exactly what we need. I like her designs. They have a freshness, a simplicity that is brilliantly different.'

'Much of her work is ceramic sculpture, something new and hardly in our line.'

'That is the whole point, my sweet.'

She hated it when he called her that. It was the last thing he meant, that she was being sweet. To be honest she didn't know herself why she was niggling about Maureen. She had to agree her work was streets ahead of the rest.

'We want something different from the old routine casseroles, dinner sets, pomanders. Her work has simplicity of form, that's what I like, and yet the photo she showed me of the moulded sculpture of a child's head, that I must see in the actual. It could become a classic in thousands of homes. Pottery isn't just a craft, one craft, it has to grow, to expand and so must we if we want to survive. We have been specialising too much . . . not that I mean we must cease our basic forms, all the stuff you do, that's your baby.' His tone was almost condescending now, 'I see a big potential for mass production of a popular form. It's what Julie had in mind.'

They were practically the words Maureen herself had used at the interview. Helen felt too tired, too drained to argue.

'Okay. But she will have to find somewhere to live of her own. I don't want her in Julie's room.' She didn't know why she said that. She only knew she didn't want Maureen under her roof. Much to her surprise Hugh gave her a long cool look and said, 'I agree absolutely.'

Maureen's sculpture of the child's head, which Hugh had admired so much, was reproduced and taken as a sample to various customers. At first reaction was slow, in some ways it was revolutionary, different, no one could quite say why. Then suddenly there was a demand which increased daily and they were overwhelmed with orders.

She also designed ceramic jewellery which was a new venture for Kendalls. To begin with there had been problems. They couldn't quite make out why it didn't sell, then they found out. They had forgotten that pendants and so on were to be worn next to the skin or on a woollen jumper and had to have a non scratchy back! Once that was put right they went like a bomb.

She also produced composite jewellery, threading together differently designed beads and clay shapes. These had to be kept thin and small because of their weight. She had a brilliant eye for colour . . . bracelets were among the most popular line, here they had found too they had to remember not to use hanging pieces as the ceramic made an ugly clinking sound against itself or side plates at a dining table. All these things they gradually found out.

At least Helen couldn't complain Maureen was lazy. She worked all hours with no complaints. Going down to the factory from the office upstairs, she would see the dark smooth head bent close to Hugh's curls, now tinged with grey on the temples, giving him a distinguished appearance. If anything he was more handsome now than when they had met, as soon as he sensed Helen's presence, he would be gazing intently at Maureen's board.

Sometimes now she lunched in the canteen as she had when Julie was there. The three of them usually met around one o'clock to have a chat about business. Now she usually found Hugh and Maureen close together at a small table. She would draw out a chair next to him . . . as if he had not noticed her he would say to Maureen some remark, refer to something about which Helen knew nothing. The most recent occasion had been the Monday morning of Maureen's third month with them when he said,

'I think your idea for one of those new kilns is just the job, Mo . . . I'll put in a tentative order and I think you and I should go to London to choose exactly what you want.' He patted her hand and gave her a tender smile . . . the smile that had once been for Helen alone. Maureen looked at him with her great blue eyes, the enigmatic *Mona Lisa* smile

34

hovering round her full lips.

For a moment anger so suffocating rose inside Helen that she thought she must take some violent action to wipe the smile off the girl's face. How dare Hugh discuss the purchase of a kiln which she knew nothing about with an employee, and suggest she go to London to choose it.

Suddenly it wasn't the immediate fate of Kendall's pottery that concerned her — it was the Kendall marriage: hers and Hugh's.

3

In spite of the success of Maureen's sculpture — 'Boy's Head' — as it was known, business generally did not improve. Everyone seemed to be in the doldrums, uncertain, cautious where spending money was concerned. Her other designs weren't selling either and a lot of money had been spent on equipment and materials, much of which had simply been wasted. Silly little things started to niggle Helen, youngsters who had come into the office didn't seem to appreciate the value of anything. She found a typist writing a note on a printed compliment slip when a scrap of paper would have done, and flew at her.

'Don't you know the value of money, of paper and printing?' The girl had given her a cool look as if she were slightly round the bend. But Helen had memories of working twenty-four hours round the clock to try to survive . . . somehow the lovely team spirit had gone out of everything with Julie leaving and the coming of Maureen; yes, she blamed it all on her.

During breakfast one morning she said to Hugh, 'I don't know if we made the right choice with Maureen. It seems now that 'Boy's Head' has more or less run its course and she's run out of ideas. Maybe she is just a little too avant-garde for the kind of market we produce for.'

He threw down his copy of the newspaper, 'Well why the hell didn't you say so at the time? You seemed perfectly satisfied with her work, you were delighted with the sculpture.'

'I know. I'm as much to blame as anyone, I'm not trying to get out of my responsibility over the whole idea, but perhaps it was a one off thing, this often happens with people, specially when they are young.'

'Good God, she's not a teenager!' He

dropped his eyes as he spoke. She wondered briefly why it was so important for Maureen's age to be mentioned, was it in case he should be accused of baby snatching? She gave herself a mental shake, she had no reason, no real reason, to think Hugh was treating the girl as anything but an employee — albeit a favoured one, but so he had Julie. That had been different, that was more a father/daughter relationship. She was sure this was far from such.

Something else had been annoying her. Maureen had made no attempt to find herself a flat or bedsitter, and out of common courtesy she had had to let her have Julie's room for the time being. Now, thinking she might as well be hung for a sheep as a lamb, she said,

'I'd be glad if you would have a word with her about finding herself some accommodation, there must be lots of places, not necessarily in the village, Tormouth isn't too far away.'

It so happened that Maureen was

away for the weekend which had given Helen the opportunity to broach the subject. The cottage wasn't all that big and now it seemed, when Maureen was there in the evenings, as if there was nowhere Helen could go to be alone, except her bedroom, and she didn't see why she should spend her evenings there. Many times she stayed on at the pottery, tidying the shop, going round the displays and altering them although it wasn't necessary, the girl who ran it was highly efficient.

Hugh got to his feet so violently his chair fell backwards.

'You are getting quite impossible at times, Helen.'

She knew she had gone too far, and yet she felt justified. He turned away and went over to the window, his shoulders hunched. Suddenly, with a completely unexpected change of mood, she felt sorry for him, a deep maternal kind of pity over the fact that things had gone wrong. He had had such high hopes as she had, and yet somehow he seemed less able to cope with the crisis they had encountered.

She got up too and went over to where he stood, stretching out her hand towards him. Sensing her presence, he turned, his face ravished.

'I know it's difficult for you to believe, but it is for you, for you and Gail that I want success. I'm not entirely selfish and unfeeling, as you seem to think. I don't mean to appear totally unsympathetic, but you must admit that sometimes you yourself are insensitive.'

Without waiting for her to comment, almost as if he were ashamed of having shown he was vulnerable, he turned towards the stairs and ran up them two at a time. It was then again the sudden pain stabbed at her chest, as if someone turned a knife. She gasped for breath, her hand flying to her throat. She felt as if she were suffocating . . . she tried to call Hugh, but no sound came from her lips. She managed to stagger to a chair, she lay back, her eyes closed. There must be something wrong more than just her age, something serious, and yet at a time like this she could not possibly afford to be ill, for so many reasons.

Gradually the pain subsided, and she dared to draw some deep breaths. She had broken out in a cold sweat, it was as if she had run up a long flight of stairs.

Slowly she got up and took the dishes to the sink. She couldn't bring herself to tell Hugh of her fears, afraid he would think she was putting on an act to gain his sympathy.

It was Sunday and as was his usual habit, Hugh went to the local pub as soon as it opened, staying there till closing time. Sometimes Helen would join him, but this morning she felt too tired, drained, it was all she could do to cook the lunch.

Much to her surprise, within a few days Maureen came to her to say she had found a tiny cottage at the other end of the village; someone had converted an old barn, she was buying it on a mortgage which Hugh had guaranteed . . .

'I'm so glad, I'm sure you'll be much happier with a place of your own.' Helen smiled at her. The girl gave her a curious look.

'Perhaps,' was all she said. Later, when she had finished packing her few belongings, she said,

'It's partly furnished, the bare necessities, quite pleasant actually, but I'd be awfully grateful if you'd give me some advice about details. The curtains are pretty grotty. Yours, and the bed linen are so nice, I love the duvet in my room.'

Helen was both surprised and overcome and she said almost before she had thought, 'Then please take it with you my dear. It won't do if ever Julie and Brough come to stay because I shall have to put a double bed in there.'

'Oh I didn't mean . . . '

Impulsively Helen put out her hand, 'No, I know you didn't, but you are most welcome to it.'

At Maureen's invitation she went to the cottage. It was really charming, it had been converted without taking away its character. There was one big room downstairs with an open fire-place, a tiny kitchen one end beautifully equipped, stairs led up to the bedroom and a minute shower room. Cupboards had been built in to the thick walls so that very little furniture was needed. Maureen had bought a sofa and a deep armchair covered in natural linen with brightly coloured cushions. The floor was already carpeted from wall to wall in dark brown.

'Very sensible,' Helen remarked, 'when the lane outside turns to winter mud.'

For a moment she was tempted to confide in Maureen about the spasms of pain and breathlessness she had, but she changed her mind. The girl could hardly be expected to have sympathy for someone who was obviously middle aged, and she probably had her own problems to solve. Whether she had a boy friend or not Helen had no idea. She had the feeling that however long you were with Maureen you would never really know her, at least not in any way she did not intend . . . and yet on the surface she was friendly enough.

Helen had brought some pieces of china and glass with her which she thought would look well in the little cottage, a rug and some bulbs in a brass bowl.

'You are very kind, it looks quite homey already,' Maureen said. For some reason it didn't to Helen, and yet she could not say why she felt thus.

Hugh took no interest in the cottage at all. When she asked him if he were going down to see it he shrugged his shoulders and said shortly,

'I might, but it's what Maureen does at work that interests me, not where she lives.' He gave Helen a long cool look as he spoke.

4

As the months passed and spring came, business did pick up a little. Maureen had designed some charming small rabbits and baby chicks for the Easter market. Helen had been surprised for they were far more conventional than her usual work; they sold tolerably well. She herself had been feeling too limp to design anything and had another blazing row with Hugh after which he had moved his things into the room in which Julie had slept.

'I can't sleep if you will keep the light on half the night reading.'

'At least you might have a little sympathy for the fact that I can't sleep.'

'Take some tablets then like other people have to.'

And so it had gone on. Sometimes she just looked at him, hardly able to believe this was the man she had married. She felt lonely, lost. Gail was busy at College and Julie half a world away. How she longed for her cheery smile, the laughs they had had together. Often now in her solitary room she lay half the night weeping into her pillow so that when the dawn broke at last she was hollow-eyed and weary. Her skin felt scaly, her hair a mess. She knew she wasn't pulling her weight, that in some way Hugh was justified in his anger with her, but it seemed impossible to pull herself back from the slough of despondency into which she had sunk.

Then one day he came back from London with an even bigger bombshell.

'I've been to see the merchant bank who run the rural industries group down here, they lend money to projects which they think are worthwhile,' he paused and gave a lopsided grin, 'and sometimes to those who aren't, I suspect, from the list I've seen.'

Helen wondered wearily what on earth was coming, surely he didn't intend to borrow some money, to mortgage more property.

'Some time ago I was driving across the moor on my way to Cornwall and I saw this place . . . a foundry where a chap makes wrought iron, the other end of the building houses a pottery. He had been working in a smithy, doing conventional jobs, shoeing horses, mending farm machinery, making gates, that kind of thing, but he's an artist as well and he decided to set up on his own and take pupils, students, at weekends, to teach them to make all kinds of things in wrought iron — lamp standards, coffee tables and so on. His work is really exquisite. There is also a place where a girl has been teaching pottery, just the rudiments, you know the old wheel bit all the amateurs like to try their hand at. She does weekend schools too, but she's getting married and husband doesn't much fancy her working so that part of the premises will be empty.'

He stopped, seeing the expression on Helen's face.

'You don't mean . . . you haven't

been to the bank to borrow money, more money to buy this place surely?'

'No, not to buy, but I've got a loan to go into partnership with Mike Tasker, that's the chap's name. I thought we could take over the pottery, we need only go up there weekends. Perhaps you and Maureen could take it in turns. We'll get some kind of cook or warden in, it's self service, like a Youth Hostel, bunk beds etc.'

Helen sank heavily on to the window seat which happened to be the nearest available place. She dropped her head into her hands, the whole prospect filled her with horror. Hugh came over and sat beside her, putting his arm along her shoulders. The first time he had touched her for months. It brought her a moment of comfort.

'Look love, you have to speculate to accumulate, you know Jules always said that. It's a wonderful spot in the heart of the moor, that alone attracts people, the peace and tranquillity, on top of the chance to express creativity. It's the in-thing now. The place stands back from the road, used to be an old powdermill, gunpowder, got quite a story. They used to use the stuff in all the quarries on the moor before dynamite was invented, and in the tin mines, the farmers used to blast the huge rocks, clear their land with it. Then when dynamite was invented the whole thing collapsed.'

Helen was hardly aware of what he said. His voice went on,

'Mike's dead keen but he needs a bit of help. All the facilities are there, a lot of fresh water, electricity, bottled gas tanks.' He got to his feet. 'Tell you what, come along and have a look at it now, a breath of fresh air will do you good anyway.'

She hadn't the strength to argue. He pushed her into the passenger seat of the car. She sat accepting the inevitable. Had Hugh taken leave of his senses? As he drove he went on talking about the old powder mill.

'The workers used to walk to work,

miles, some of them. Then their wives would bring their lunch to the gates. They had to stop there, weren't allowed inside because of the danger of explosion. There was one very bad accident, several people killed. Then of course word went round it was haunted. It stood empty for years. There's a quite nice house there, belonged to the manager, where Mike lives, only wants a bit doing to it, and a cottage and the forge, some huts where the weekend students stay.' As he spoke he turned off the moorland road along a tarmac track which was full of potholes.

'Have to do something to this, otherwise people won't risk their springs.'

Now he pointed to a small cannon standing beside the track. 'That's the old mortar they used to test the gunpowder.'

In spite of her feelings, Helen looked round with interest. It was a beautiful early summer day without enough wind to stir a cobweb, and as usual the moors, the distant tors, the smell of the turf and the sound of the larks acted as a kind of soporific on her nerves. She had always loved the moor but never seemed to have enough time to spend there. The sky was an upturned bowl of blue above them as Hugh brought the car to a standstill in front of a granite slate-roofed cottage, a small glass porch jutted out in front, the paint was peeling, but the place looked sturdy as though it was built to stand the worst that winter could throw at it.

She got out of the car and the breeze which had suddenly arisen, tugged at her hair, it was fresh and fragrant on her face, the smell of gorse which always reminded her of fresh apricots filled her nostrils. Some distance away stood a half ruined chimney, she supposed part of the remains of the powder factory itself. Somewhere she could hear the clang of metal on metal and a strong voice lifted in the latest pop song. There was the smell of smoke and tar and paraffin all mixed up with the moorland perfumes. She closed her eyes for a moment listening to the lark as it spiralled up into the blue. Quite inconsequently she thought, I could be happy here. A small door led into the living accommodation for the students. Hugh pushed it open. It was a long room with high windows, some rather tatty chairs, a table, a dartboard and at the far end, some bunks stood against one wall.

'It needs a bit of work done on it, I thought Maureen could spend some time here.' He walked on through another door where there was a small kitchen, quite well equipped with a bottled gas cooker, a sink, and plenty of storage cupboards. Beyond that a row of showers.

'Not exactly the Ritz, but when people come up on the moor they don't expect the height of luxury. It's a working weekend.'

Helen felt very strange, almost as if she had come home, although the surroundings were hardly conducive. It was something about the atmosphere, slightly raffish as it was, it still had a warmth, a feeling of continuity.

'Is the powdermill itself very old?'

Hugh swung round. It was the first time she had spoken.

'I think so, not quite sure how old. Mike may be able to tell you.' As he spoke a tall dark haired man in a leather apron came through the door.

'Hullo Hugh. How are you? Can't shake hands, I'm filthy.' Catching sight of Helen he went on, 'Beg pardon, Missis . . . '

Helen smiled. For some reason she was reminded of Weyland Smith the legendary blacksmith.

'This is my wife, Helen . . . Mike Tasker,' Hugh made the introductions. Mike nodded, spreading out his hands and grinning apologetically.

'I was just trying to explain to Helen about the old powdermill. I know you are an expert on its history.'

Mike smiled down at her. He must

have been over six and a half feet tall.

'Don't know all that much really. When I was a nipper Dad used to bring me here for a walk and tell me about it. Even then I longed to live here, never thought I'd do it this way though. They made the powder by mixing sulphur, saltpetre and charcoal and they had to be ground very fine. The millstones were hard border rock rather than granite.' He pointed through the door, sections of the old millstones could be seen as paving. Helen could have listened to him for hours with his lovely Devon burr. 'They used to test the powder by firing a shot over a measured range from that old mortar up there. Some of it was taken to the Cornish slate quarries at Delabole.'

He broke off and pointed through the windows, 'See those alder trees? They were planted round the mill to provide a wind break and wood suitable to make into charcoal which they needed to make the old black powder.'

He turned back, looking at Helen again. ' 'Twas a dangerous job and they had many accidents. They built most of the cottages for the workers at some distance from the mill, out on the turnpike road. It was the manager and foreman, and men with special tasks lived here,' he pointed along the row of buildings, 'the manager had the posh one with the porch! That's where I live now, and another of the cottages was used as a day school and Sunday chapel.'

Helen was becoming more and more fascinated. She had forgotten her worries, her anger with Hugh, she could understand his wanting to be part of this.

'About a hundred years ago they closed the mills, dynamite was invented in 1869 by a chap called Nobel.'

'How is it you know so much about it?' Helen asked him, smiling.

'Well my great great granddad worked here. Quite a character he was I'm told. To show how dangerous it was, he carried his breakfast and dinner to work and ate both at breakfast time less he should be blown up. Didn't like waste! Some of the wives brought a hot pasty for their men, but had to wait at the gate, entrance was strictly forbidden.'

Helen went out on to the paved walk which ran in front of the terrace of little cottages, and the house. The whole place had captured her imagination and it was as if Mike himself were part of the fabric of the place. She left him and Hugh discussing the various business plans. She couldn't quite make up her mind if she were glad or sorry about the new partnership.

5

In spite of her enjoyment of the visit to the powdermills, there was the realisation of the flagging business of their own pottery. For the time being Hugh was leaving Mike to continue his work with a few students at weekends, but a lot was going to have to be done to make it more attractive. As the weeks passed and the memory of that golden afternoon faded, the relationship between Helen and Hugh seemed to deteriorate. He would pick on her over the smallest details — she had tried to work on some new designs for the summer tourist trade, but everything seemed banal, ordinary. There was no inspiration. Finally Hugh said one evening as they finished supper,

'We can't go on like this can we? It's tearing us both apart. I can't concentrate on my work, and it's quite obvious you can't.' He got up and started to fill his pipe, not looking at her. 'I think the best thing would be for us to part for a while, a kind of trial separation, give us both a chance to readjust, living under the same roof just doesn't seem possible, as well as working together.'

Although in some ways his words were not a complete surprise, she felt deeply hurt and resentful. She had given so much to the business, tried to make a home, to bring up Gail, and this was all it had amounted to — a handful of ashes. Perhaps if she hadn't been so tired, so drained, she wouldn't have spoken as she did, because she regretted the words almost as soon as they left her lips. But they were said. They could not be recalled.

'I suppose you're in love with that girl Maureen! I've suspected it all along!'

He didn't reply for a moment, making much of the business of lighting his pipe, then,

'I hadn't thought much about it.

Perhaps I am. I certainly like her, she's good company, which is more than can be said for you these days.'

Helen could have bitten out her tongue, but she knew it was too late, too late to apologise even. The words hung between them like letters of fire.

'Then if that's the way you feel, there isn't much alternative,' she said quietly, all passion spent now.

He put the dead matches carefully in the ashtray.

'Right. Then I'll try to find somewhere.'

Once again bitter anger rose inside her.

'You can't go to Rose Cottage — Maureen's place . . . there's only a single bed.' She knew her voice was full of spite and it was such a stupid, trite remark.

'I had no intention of doing any such thing, all this is in your own mind,' he said coolly.

Suddenly the most incredible idea struck her. Probably she was mad to suggest it, and yet in many ways it was a solution, to get the quiet, the privacy she longed for.

'To save you the trouble of looking, I'll go,' she said quietly.

'You? I thought you were so attached to this house . . . couldn't bear the thought of leaving it.'

'A great deal of what it meant to me — to us — has gone away. After all it is only a house, not a home,' she said slowly.

'Where the hell would you go?'

'Up on the moor. To the powdermill. I could be the one to act as warden, head cook and bottle washer at week-ends. It would still give me time to come down here to the pottery, maybe I could even take my things up there and design, after all there is everything needed — a small kiln, a wheel, storage space.'

He stood looking at her. 'You can't be serious.'

'I've probably never been so serious about anything in my whole life.' The more she thought about it the more she liked the idea, but first of all she had to approach Mike, ask him if he minded, after all it was his territory.

She drove up one clear summer day. When she arrived he was having problems with a leaking oil tank and was smothered from head to foot in smelly diesel. He grinned at her, his teeth white in an almost black face.

'Mike, I won't take a moment of your time, but I am thinking of coming up here to stay for a little while, to look after the students at the weekends. Would you mind?'

He looked at her for a moment as if he thought she were slightly off her head. She had to laugh at the expression on his face.

'I know it sounds a bit odd, but I do need peace and quiet. I've been a bit under the weather,' she dropped her gaze, wondering if he realised things were not too good between herself and Hugh, 'and this seems just what I need. I promise not to make a nuisance of myself.'

He rubbed his hands down his apron as if lost for words.

'I'd be honoured, Missis. It's pretty lonely in the week when all the folk are gone, though I have plenty of work. It seems to have picked up lately, people want wrought iron both inside and outside their houses these days.'

'Then that's fine. I'll be moving in shortly. I want a bit of decorating done inside the cottage, I thought I'd use the one which used to be the school down in the dip there.'

He nodded, 'A good choice, but of course you should really have the one I live in, used to be the manager's.'

'I'm not the manager, just another employee, and warden,' she grinned. She hadn't felt quite so light hearted for a long time — no — perhaps that was not quite the word. She couldn't feel that while the position remained as it was between herself and Hugh, but at least now she had a purpose.

It was fun furnishing the little cottage, arranging for a local man to paint the walls and woodwork, to bring up some of her favourite paintings and bit of china and furniture. Hugh was going to stay in their own cottage. She had arranged for a woman to come in and cook and clean for him.

'I can eat out,' he said shortly, not meeting her eyes.

It was the end of June before she managed to get everything arranged. They had advertised the facilities they were offering and she had done quite a lot of work on the living quarters for the students, managed to get a woman to come from the nearby village to help with the cooking — good wholesome country food which people seemed to appreciate as much as the unusual course Mike offered. For the moment she hadn't started the pottery courses, she had enough on her plate, but she was almost happy again. Almost.

Inevitably the gossips were busy in a small village and it wasn't long before they made it their business to let her know. Maureen and Hugh were seen everywhere together. The precious life she had been trying to build up again, hoping that time would heal the rift between them, that the parting would prove to be such sweet sorrow that he would come back to her . . . all was shattered, even the peace and tranquillity of the powdermill now could not bring her comfort as she lay on the narrow bed, sobbing . . . and then once more the knife pierced her chest . . . she struggled for breath . . . whispering his name as the needles of sharp summer rain beat a tattoo on the little window of the cottage, and she felt as grey and hopeless as the sky which hung low over the tors.

6

Helen told herself it was a well known fact that when you reached the nadir, the time of greatest depression, there was only one way ahead, and that was up.

She had fallen asleep although she had thought the pain too intense to allow such a thing. When she opened her eyes the rain had stopped, and so had the pain, in fact she felt strangely refreshed. She got up and went over to the window. She must have slept for over twelve hours. There was a rain-washed dawn over the moor, a curlew gave its mournful cry, there was the lovely fresh smell of turf and gorse. She could hear the nearby leat as it ran over the stones, obviously filled by the rain, which would mean she could have a bath, for it operated an age old system through a ram in some miraculous manner which she did not understand, lifting the water up a series of wooden shutes into a huge tank. It had been a long dry summer, but still they had not been really short of water, although Michael had said they should conserve it to some extent.

Now it was nearly the end of July and holiday weeks approaching. The reaction to her advertisements in both local and national papers and magazines had borne fruit: craft weekends, tuition in pottery or wrought iron. Some people came just to watch Mike and to see the display he had built up of country tools and implements which he had collected from moorland and other farms. Many of these people were so fascinated by it all that they stayed to learn the craft, for he had also built up quite a collection of handmade items which he had produced in the smithy. Mike was a friendly person to talk to, and he was beginning to get quite a reputation for his traditional designs of balustrades, garden railings with matching gates, his biggest success being with the free-standing branched candelabra in different sizes. Sensibly he kept his prices below those in the shops.

Helen had been too absorbed in getting the cottage and the student accommodation organised to spend much time on her own work and designing, but the trickle of students was starting to become a steady stream and August promised to be a busy month. There had been one or two minor crises when the drain had got blocked with liquid clay and she had had to get Michael to help her. He had made a grating to go over it with a trap, easy to clean out so it wouldn't happen again. 'How would I ever manage without you?' she had said, thanking him.

He had grinned 'I reckon none of us is indispensable, Missis.'

'Maybe but some less than others,' she replied.

Now she went into the tiny bathroom which she had had built off her bedroom. The brown peaty water was hot, the benison of its softness relaxed her. She lay in the warmth, thinking of Hugh, somehow she had to come to terms with the situation between them. She had had high hopes of this trial separation, that at least he would miss her, but that had been a fantasy world perhaps. It seemed he was managing quite well without her, she had even heard that business had improved a little now she was not there.

She spent practically all her time now at the Powdermill. The peace and tranquillity of the place had seeped into her. Perhaps she would eventually even come to terms with the fact that she had to live without Hugh, forget the past and make a new life. But there was still a raw wound inside her every time she thought of him with Maureen, her imagination putting them into all kinds of situations, intimate, warm, loving which had once been just between herself and Hugh. Quickly she would try to dismiss them, go out on the moor, whatever the weather.

To her great joy she had found a nearby source of clay which she had dug up and experimented with, taking a few pounds and testing it for plasticity. She rolled coils and tied them like a ring around her finger. It didn't crack, it was malleable, plastic. She rolled some out into slabs and made tiny dishes and bowls, cut some tiles and bisque fired them in the old kiln, mixing in some 'grog', pre-fired high temperature clay which she bought pulverised in different degrees of coarseness.

Some of it she weathered, spreading it in the sun and wind and rain, turning it over to expose fresh surfaces. She somehow experienced a new feeling over the actual manual work involved. Before she had always bought her clay. Often now too she worked without the wheel, handbuilding, getting an enormous satisfaction out of it, encouraging students to do the same.

'The point is you can do this

anywhere, in a garden shed, or a spare room, even the kitchen when you don't need a wheel.' She started them off with simple moulds using old worn out wooden salad bowls, rolling out the clay with a rolling pin . . . they were thrilled when they found out how simple it was. Some of the work they decorated, carving designs in the centre or outside walls, finding a deep content in the simple, ancient craft and its unlimited creative potential.

To Helen it was a kind of relief, a relaxation after the struggle always to create something new and original. Anyone could do this, making old salad bowls, ashtrays, cracked soup plates come back to new and splendid variations. Some of them built up bowls with thin, leaf-like slabs or coiled a pot with long snakes of clay, attaching them one after another to form the walls of a pot. She discovered herself that the whole secret of handbuilding was a relaxed pace, and this was doing her more good than anything.

Sometimes she would spend half an hour, when the students had gone, walking round the shelves the carpenter had built for her round the main hut, carrying their work. Although they had been coming only a few weeks, already it looked like a small gallery.

She didn't see much of Michael, he too was busy and absorbed. She would hear the ring of his hammer, the hiss of red hot metal as it was plunged into cold water. Sometimes she asked him in for a meal during the week, weekends were too busy. He was a man of few words, but always expressed great appreciation of her cooking.

'My Mum was a good cook, but we were bone poor. Dad worked in the tin mines at one time but they closed and there was nothing else he knew. Got some seasonal work on farms, but most of the moor is grazing, try to grow corn or hay the moor will break your heart — and your back. You only got to go and look at any of they newtakes which someone once tried to cultivate

71

— moor soon takes over.'

His uncle had been a blacksmith in a small village in north Devon, but during the war had joined up and his smithy had closed. 'I remember when I was a tacker watching him shoe the shires, lifting up their great hooves by the hair . . . that was what decided me, though I wanted something more than just horses pretty soon. Course they come back into fashion with show jumping, eventing and so on. I made a living,' he paused . . .

'But you had the artistic gift, designing . . . I wonder where that came from,' Helen said.

He shook his head, 'Goodness knows. Though my gran used to talk of Spanish blood from the time of the Armada, 'tis said some of the sailors from the wrecked ships stayed to wed our little maids . . . maybe that's where I get the ideas . . . I seen some of the wrought iron they make in Spain, said to have been brought from Morocco.'

Their talk was easy, familiar, but

never intimate, it was a growing friendship which Helen greatly valued.

But none of it resolved the situation with Hugh. Gail was due back from College, she had passed her exams and there had been some openings available for jobs, she had a couple of weeks free at the beginning of August and Helen knew she was going to have to explain the position to her. Up to now she had simply told her that Hugh had invested some money in a new venture on the moor which she was supervising, she had made no mention of their separation or of Maureen. It was going to be a difficult explanation to give, Gail adored her father and had always been the apple of his eye. Somehow Helen was going to have to put the situation to her without allotting blame; it would not be easy.

The occasion arose sooner than she had anticipated. A letter came for her from Gail, sent on from the cottage. The girl said she had got herself a holiday job in Plymouth, working in a bar on the Barbican, just to fill in. She was going to pop home first for a couple of days and looking forward to relaxing . . . exciting news . . . Alan has been offered a job . . . but more of this when I see you.

Helen took the letter out on to the little square of grass outside the cottage and perched on the stone wall. The peace and tranquillity of the moor enfolded her, the sky was an upturned bowl of blue . . . How did you tell a beloved daughter, who worshipped her father, and was fond of her mother too, that the secure background she had known all her childhood had suddenly dissolved like a sandcastle on the beach? She knew a young person's whole outlook on life, their future behaviour could be affected by something like this. Gail had always been such a home-lover, so proud of her close knit family.

She wondered briefly what job Alan had been offered. He and Gail had been engaged for about six months.

74

Helen liked him very much, although he was the least likely man she would ever have thought Gail would fall for; an accountant, practical and prosaic, perhaps a tiny bit dull, he was probably quite different when he and Gail were alone togeher. She had felt he wanted to be sure to make a good impression on Helen and Hugh. Gail had explained he came from a broken home, had been brought up by various aunts, and was worried, knowing how close Gail's parents were, that they might doubt his own reliability as a husband.

Helen sighed as she thought of him. The boot was certainly on the other foot now, although Gail had no idea of it. Both she and Hugh had always thought Alan was the ideal husband for their daughter who sometimes was intrepid, Alan would keep her feet on the ground. His firm, where he had been apprenticed thought very highly of him and foretold a brilliant future.

She got up. She would have to do

something about making sure Gail knew where to come and look for her. She had better ring Mrs Riley who was looking after the cottage and ask her to leave a message . . .

It was Sunday evening and most of the students were packing up their belongings. It had been a busy week, they had had a wonderful time digging their own clay, preparing it — some of them had been learning to glaze. Helen had made sure Mrs Pearse, the woman who came to help with the cooking, provided plenty of food — potting seemed to be a great appetite raiser! She wanted to make sure they felt they had had their money's worth.

Her interest in the students made the time pass quickly, she had little opportunity to brood. She tried not to show favouritism which wasn't easy as one or two were really gifted, while some, however hard they tried, could do nothing right and were all thumbs, or as one old Devon woman had once remarked, seeing someone struggling helplessly with a task . . . ' 'Er be like a cow with a musket.'

She waved the last of the students off and turned back with relief to make herself a cup of tea when she saw a small car bumping its way along the tarmac road. Surely it couldn't be anyone for her, perhaps for Michael, she had on an old shapeless pair of slacks and one of Hugh's shirts. Her hair needed washing. With mounting horror she saw the car had passed Michael's cottage and was approaching hers, it drew up and Gail jumped out. She ran to her mother and flung her arms round her neck.

'Darling how wonderful to see you, but I thought it was next week.' She'd had no time to ring Mrs Riley. How on earth had Gail found her? How much did she know?

Arms entwined, they went into the cottage. 'I'm afraid it's all a bit primitive still, I was just going to make a cuppa . . . ' She couldn't think what to say . . .

'What on earth is going on, Mum?' There was nothing dreamy about Gail now, her face was pale, tense, her eyes shadowed. 'I went to the cottage and there was some strange woman there cleaning the cooker. I thought at first something terrible had happened. Why on earth didn't you let me know? She told me you were out here on the moor, at some powdermill or something. I hadn't a clue what she was talking about. I asked her what time you would be back . . . she gave me a very old fashioned look and said she had no idea . . . 'Best look for your Dad at Miss Maureen's' she said, looking disapproving, sniffed, and that was that. For a moment I thought I'd flipped my lid and gone to the wrong address . . . or she'd flipped hers.'

Helen turned off the kettle, put tea bags in the cups, playing for time. She had rehearsed what she was going to say through the long watches of the night, now her throat had dried up. Gail followed her round the kitchen, her high heeled sandals clicking on the slate floor as if they demonstrated her disapproval. Helen poured the tea, added milk and sugar, pushed a plate of biscuits along the scrubbed table top. Gail's mouth was drooping in a well remembered way from her childhood. The prelude to tears, obvious she had guessed most of the story. She sat heavily on the hard wooden chair.

'Honestly I don't know where to begin, in fact I don't know exactly what happened, what is going to happen. I only know a time came when I had to be alone, somehow to assess the situation, have time to think, and when Hugh took up this partnership with Michael here, it seemed a good idea.' When said like that it sounded so weak, ineffectual, not what she had meant to say.

'Who's Michael?' Gail's brow was furrowed. It was the last remark Helen had expected.

'The chap who runs the forge. I told you, Hugh's in partnership with him.'

Gail kicked off her sandals, dismissing Michael for the time. Helen went on slowly, 'I suppose as in every situation like this both people are to blame, six of one, half a dozen of the other. Perhaps even I should take a larger part of it because I recommended Maureen, she seemed a good choice, although we can never replace Julie.'

Gail nodded and said with a touch of impatience, 'We all agree on that, so?'

'She's good at her job, I have to admit that. She brought in new business with her 'Boy's Head', but that dropped off in time.' She paused a moment, 'your father . . . ' Oh God, had it come to speaking of Hugh like that . . . She swallowed and then went on, 'business was bad, I think that got on top of both of us. We've given so much of our lives, our youth, everything, to building it up. Maureen is a good designer, I don't deny that, but she is too ambitious, too avant-garde for our kind of trade in this area . . . '

'Mum!' Gail interrupted her mother, 'I'm not interested at the moment in the business or this girl Maureen, all I want to know is what is happening between you and Dad, my family.'

Helen lifted her head now and looked at her daughter, 'It's a temporary situation . . . separation, at the moment. I just felt I had to get away, to be alone. Try to understand. I know it's difficult. But I knew he was . . . well . . . interested in this girl. The two of them made me feel like an outsider, an intruder almost in my own home, my own business, in so many ways. Somehow I had to try to get the whole thing in the right perspective. She's young, not much older than you, lively, gifted, and I . . . well . . .' she was determined at this juncture not to burden Gail with her own ill health . . . 'I have to admit I'm not as young as I was, I get tired, lose interest to some extent, not exactly the life and soul of the party.' She tried to grin but it was a tight-lipped travesty.

Gail shot her a keen glance, 'You're

not actually ill are you Mum? You look a bit peaky and I'm sure you're working too hard here.'

Helen dropped her gaze, 'No I'm fine really. I do get a bit tired, but I enjoy the work as much as I've ever done anything. I like meeting people, people who are interested in the same things that I am, who I can help. It's lovely watching them develop, find their own potential, that they can do things they never thought they could. Specially the women, once they find out there's no stopping them.'

'All that isn't really the point,' her voice was impatient, 'I just can't believe Dad would flip his lid over a girl, jeopardise his marriage . . . the family, our home. You've always been so close, to me the ideal marriage, something I thought I could model my own on. I always felt I was so lucky to be brought up with such a background. Most of my friends at school and college seem to have broken homes or some problem, unstable backgrounds, even Alan . . . I just can't believe now I'm the same as all the others.' Her voice broke and tears started to pour down her cheeks. Helen got up and put her arms round her, drawing her head on to her breast, comforting her as she had done when she was a small girl and grazed her knee or broken a beloved doll.

'Hush darling, it's not the end of the world. These things happen, and pass. Men of your father's age do go through a kind of male menopause, odd as it may seem. It is talked about more these days.' She paused a moment, trying to find words to lighten the tenseness, 'At least it can't be the seven year itch! We must have passed through that phase years ago!' she sounded a little rueful, 'perhaps that's part of the trouble. We have been so busy, the years have drifted by, melted like snow before the sun. Where did they go? Perhaps we haven't had the time to spend together that we should. We were so anxious to make a go of the business, to make a home for you, perhaps that's where we went wrong.' She was speaking to herself as much as to her daughter now.

Gradually the girl's sobs decreased. Her mother was giving her a little feeling of reassurance as she always did. She dried her eyes and blew her nose.

'I could kill that wretched girl, even though we haven't met yet!'

Helen grinned, 'You might even like her. Probably I would myself under different conditions.'

'Dad ought to be ashamed of himself. I'm going down to the cottage, or the pottery tomorrow, wherever I can find him, and tell him what I think of him — both of them.'

'Oh no you won't,' Helen said quickly, 'this is something Hugh and I have to work out ourselves, even you can't help there, my poppet.' Suddenly she realised how easily Hugh's pet name for his daughter had rolled off her lips. Gail squeezed her hand reassuringly as if she had realised the same thing. Helen felt the tears now behind her own lids at the show of affection and sympathy, something she had not experienced lately.

'Look, let's forget all this for a moment and talk about you, you and Alan.'

Gail drew in her breath quickly. 'Of course, I'd forgotten, that was really the whole purpose of the enterprise, as they say. I came to talk to you and Dad. You know we are engaged of course, well we're hoping to get married sooner than we had anticipated.'

Helen was taken aback, Alan had been so definite that he wanted everything to be just right, cut and dried, a house bought and so on before they actually married. That was why Gail had gone on with her studies and her career, to help save enough money.

'As you know, Alan is qualified now — well any moment. And the people he's been apprenticed to have offered him a super job in one of their own branches . . .'

'Darling that's marvellous . . . where?'

Gail looked down for a moment,

turning her engagement ring round and round, then she said, 'Melbourne, Australia . . . '

For a moment there was a dead silence. Helen heard a fly buzzing in a web somewhere . . . Australia . . . Julie and now Gail. Why did everyone have to go to the other side of the world, the people she loved and needed? Once more tears rose behind her lids, but she brushed them away. Nothing must spoil her daughter's joy.

'Well darling, it's a long way, but if it's a good job and it's what you both want . . . '

'Oh Mum it's no distance these days with jet travel. You'll be able to hop over, you and Dad, when he comes to his senses.' There was a pleading note in her tone.

Helen tried to keep her own voice normal. 'How soon . . . ?'

'Just before Christmas. I didn't want a winter wedding, I'd have liked a summer one like Julie, but I haven't much choice, I'm not letting him go alone.'

'Of course.' The idea of Gail miles away filled her with dread.

'Well that's what I came to tell you, to ask if we could make the arrangements, perhaps for the end of November. That's why I've taken this temporary job in Plymouth, to save a bit of money, and the firm said if we like to buy some of the furniture and things we need, they'll pay for the transport. They'll fix us up with a house out there too. It's a wonderful chance.'

For a moment Helen felt too overwhelmed with the thought of losing Gail, of all the arrangements that had to be made in the next few weeks ... she'd only just recovered from Julie's ... her mind boggled too at the compromise of some sort she and Hugh would have to come to. However she was determined Gail should not be aware of this.

'Come on then, I'll show you the tiny room where you'll sleep, there's lots to be done to the cottage still, but I think it'll be nice when it's finished.'

'But Mum you're not going to stay here that long are you?'

Fortunately for Helen she didn't have to reply for at that moment Michael appeared in the doorway, seeing Gail he hesitated.

'I'm sorry Mrs Kendall, I thought all the students had gone.'

'So they have, this is my daughter, Gail . . . remember I said she'd be down for a few days, well it's a lovely surprise, she turned up sooner than I thought.'

He grinned at Gail and held out his hand. 'It is fairly clean but I'm afraid a blacksmith never has lily white hands.'

Gail took his hand, feeling the firm grip, 'I know, the world's workers have other things to think about.'

'Well I hope to see you tomorrow perhaps, Miss Kendall, I'd like to show you the forge.'

She nodded, 'Gail, please, I don't like formality, and I'd love to see some of your work.'

When he'd gone she turned to her mother, 'Mm, he's dishy. I could almost fancy him myself . . . '

Helen was relieved at least she seemed to have recovered a little from her shock over herself and Hugh.

Gail was delighted with the tiny room. 'It's lovely, I like the Laura Ashley theme,' she bounced up and down on the bed, 'comfy I guess. Shan't need the duvet but thank goodness blankets have gone out of fashion before I have to buy any — at least I suppose they're with it enough in Aussie land to have heard of duvets, although maybe not with all those sheep!'

Helen rang Hugh at the office the next morning. It was strange to hear his voice, he sounded surprised and a little apprehensive.

'It's O.K. No special crisis, but Gail's home for a few days and naturally would like to see you. She and Alan are thinking of getting married before Christmas.'

'Oh my God,' he broke in, 'nothing . . . there's nothing . . . well . . . wrong?'

'If you mean is she pregnant,

certainly not!' Helen's tone was sharp. There was a time when Hugh wouldn't even have thought such a thing, about his daughter, let alone voiced it.

'It's simply that Alan has a good job offered him in Australia, and naturally she wants to go with him.' She couldn't resist the temptation to tell him the bald facts without sugaring the pill. She felt he deserved some pain for all he had caused her.

'I have to go to London for a couple of days, can she make it Thursday — can you both make it then?'

'I should think so. We'll see you at the cottage about half past nine in the morning. She's got a part-time job in Plymouth to make a bit of extra cash for all the things they'll need.'

'There's no necessity for that. I'll give her a cheque!'

'I don't think you'll find that's quite the point,' Helen said quietly. 'Anyway we can discuss all that when we see you.' As she put the receiver down her hand was shaking so much she dropped it on to its cradle.

She and Gail spent the next couple of days 'doing the rounds' as Helen described it. In spite of the forthcoming meeting with Hugh, which she was dreading, she felt more lighthearted than she had for weeks. It was so lovely having her daughter. Only now and then when she thought of the coming parting did she feel a wave of misery. The days were not long enough. She had an old van she drove round the fairs and markets, taking 'seconds' from the pottery, which she sold at half price for the students. Now she had quite a wide range to offer. Gail proved to be an expert saleswoman . . .

They also went 'Scavenging'. When she first explained what this was, Gail looked appalled. 'Mum it sounds like collecting trash for the dustman, you have to be joking.'

Helen smiled, 'No, really, it's good fun. We need glass jars, plastic containers, coffee cans, old cooking pots, barrels, basins, ladels, spoons — everything you can think of for storing glaze and bashing clay around. I've found sandwich bars are wonderful sources for empty gallon jars . . . the spoons are for glaze mixing and application . . . and you know those wooden pallets so many of the transport firms have where fork lifts are used? They are perfect supports for stacking fifty and one hundred pound bags of clay to keep them out of the wet . . . then keep your eyes open for slate slabs from old fireplaces and so on . . . they are marvellous for display shelves.'

Gail was soon sold on the idea. They enjoyed driving around, eating a pub lunch, coming back to Powdermills for a fry up in the evening. On the last evening they invited Michael to join them for a candlelit dinner. 'It's hardly romantic in these surroundings,' Helen said, 'but we can make some kind of atmosphere and try out our pottery candlesticks at the same time . . . 'fraid we'll have to use sherry glasses for the wine, they're all we've got.'

'It'll taste just as good,' Michael said

slowly as he opened the bottle. Helen had roast a duck with all the trimmings and soft music filled the little kitchen from Gail's cassette player . . . Helen really felt a supreme moment of happiness.

She hadn't been to the cottage for several weeks. She pushed open the gate which badly needed a coat of paint. The grass needed cutting and weeds had taken over the flower beds. It plucked at her heart, for however busy she had been she always tried to keep it tidy at least. But if she was shocked at the sight of the garden, she was even more so when Hugh opened the door as he saw them coming up the path. He had certainly gone to seed. His hair needed cutting — or perhaps he's just being trendy to keep up with Maureen's age group, she thought. He was wearing a pair of jeans which were too tight and badly needed washing . . . she couldn't help a feeling of compassion which flooded through her . . . his face too troubled her. His eyes were shadowed, his mouth drooped at the corners like a small boy about to burst into tears, but when he saw Gail he opened his arms and smiled, his whole face lighting up.

'Darling, how lovely to see you, and to hear your news about the wedding . . . come along inside.' He glanced over her shoulder at Helen — his eyes beseeching understanding . . .

For a moment Gail hesitated, then she flung herself at him, crying, the tears pouring down her cheeks as she whispered, 'Oh daddy, darling darling daddy . . .'

It was at that moment someone came from the shadow of the hall, the sun glinting off her dark hair . . .

Maureen stood behind Hugh, a smirk on her face as she said . . .

'My goodness . . . what a touching family reunion . . .'

7

Maureen's words — 'What a touching family reunion . . . ' uttered with such venom and acidity, made Helen feel physically sick with anger. She knew how it would feel to want to hit out at someone, hurt them, even perhaps kill them . . . the idea frightened her, but involuntarily she lifted her hand as if she were going to strike either Maureen or Hugh . . .

Gail had drawn back from her father as if she herself had been assaulted. Hugh leant forward and grabbed his daughter's arm, pulling her into the tiny hall of the cottage. Somehow, blindly, Helen followed. There was hardly room for the four of them in such a tiny space, and for a moment they were of necessity crowded so that they touched each other, making Helen recoil — she was aware of Maureen's expensive perfume, the familiar smell of Hugh's aftershave which she always gave him for his birthday. She closed her eyes, praying she wouldn't disgrace herself by fainting, then opened them quickly, knowing she must somehow find the strength to support Gail in this sordid scene.

Maureen was the first to speak. 'Well, I'm off Hugh, see you later at the pottery, there's lots to do.' She dropped a light kiss on his cheek and without looking at either Gail or Helen, swept out of the door and they heard her high heels clicking down the brick path.

For a moment no one moved or spoke. Then Hugh said as if they were visitors, guests in the little cottage which had been home for most of their lives, in fact the only home Gail had ever known . . . 'Come along into the kitchen. I'll make some coffee.'

He turned and walked away. Gail put her arm round her mother's shoulders, she seemed to have recovered her composure more quickly than the older woman.

'Come on Mum, let's go. I don't think I want to talk to . . . him . . . ' She couldn't bring herself to say the word 'Daddy'.

Helen shook her head. 'We have to love, there are things to be discussed and arranged, things to settle between the three of us.'

'O.K. But let's make it as brief as possible.' She walked ahead now, almost striding into the kitchen as if she had the whole situation well in hand. Helen was struck by how like Hugh she was in this, it brought a fresh wave of misery. She was thankful though that both she and Gail seemed somehow to have gained control, their self confidence restored, thankful there hadn't been some kind of brawl between the four of them.

Hugh had never been much use in the kitchen, even when very occasionally she had to stay in bed with a bad bout of 'flu, the trays of food he had brought her had been what even he described as an international disaster

. . . although she had tried to swallow the runny soft boiled egg which was revolting, the half-burnt toast, or whatever he had struggled to prepare. She knew then at least it had been with love in his heart. Now he had put some milk on the stove for the coffee, and while he spooned the powder into the mugs, it boiled over with a loud hiss. Automatically Helen stepped forward to turn off the gas and saw the stove was deep in burnt on grease, stains of many kinds covered the plates and even the grill gleamed with congealed fat.

'Doesn't Mrs Riley come in?' she asked, turning to the sink to soak the saucepan. In some ways it was a relief to make such an ordinary remark in extraordinary circumstances.

Hugh raised his brows, 'Yes of course, why?'

Helen shrugged, 'She certainly hasn't spent much time on cleaning the stove!'

'Oh that! We had some people in last evening and Mo did a fry up.' Both the intimacy of the nickname, and the unaccustomed phrase on his lips — an attempt to be 'with it', made Helen wince.

There were rings on the pine table where hot liquid had spilt. She longed to get the cloth and the cleaner and start to freshen the place up, but Gail was leaning against the sink now, the mug of coffee in her hand. Hugh straddled the chair, his hands resting on the back — even that was an unnatural pose. It was like looking at a stranger, or a child who was anxious to impress the grownups with his behaviour. Once again she was torn between anger, sorrow and a great, deep compassion for this man she had loved, did still deep down love, more than life itself.

She sank down on the window seat where she had spent precious moments in the past, waiting for a meal to cook, doing some knitting or sewing, her hands never idle, for there had never been time for them to be.

'Well, so you and Alan are getting married and flying the nest!' Hugh tried to sound lighthearted, but it didn't quite come off, in fact his voice almost broke on the words. But Gail seemed to have gained a sudden maturity and she said quietly,

'Yes, we are getting married before Christmas, and have to be in Melbourne early in the New Year. We wanted a little time at least to settle in. The firm are providing a flat and the basic furniture but there will be quite a lot to do, things we shall need. That is why I decided to take a job for the next few weeks.'

Helen could see that in spite of the brave front she was putting on, her lower lip trembled. She longed to go and take her in her arms, but realised this was something — a battle of some kind, the girl had to resolve for herself.

'You know sweetheart, there isn't any need for that. Business may be bad, but at least there are a few spare pennies for my best girl, to buy the bottom drawer necessities.'

'Thank you but it's a decision Alan

and I came to before . . . ' she looked away, she had been going to say 'before I knew about all this . . . '

'Well,' he looked hopefully at Helen, but she wasn't going to throw him a lifeline just yet. 'I expect you'd like the reception at the village pub like Julie had.'

Gail glanced quickly at her mother as he spoke. Helen gave a tiny nod . . . why not . . . she wasn't going to let Maureen spoil the wedding. The village would probably make a nine days' wonder of the whole thing, and she knew their friends would rally round. The thought of having to go through the day with the situation as it was between Hugh and herself really didn't bear contemplation at the moment, but for Gail's sake it was something that had to be faced.

'Yes please I would,' she hesitated a moment, then lifting her head looked her father full in the face, 'and in spite of everything, I'd like you to give me away.'

Hugh's face seemed to crumple, to disintegrate as she spoke. Swiftly he stepped towards her and put his arm round her. Once again she buried her face in the comforting warmth and familiar smell of his coat as he said, 'Of course, darling. There would never be any question of anything else.'

Helen expected her to sob, but she lifted her face like a small girl waiting to be kissed, and he bent and did so on her lips. Then she drew away as if she could not trust herself to say any more. Helen glanced at her watch, 'We ought to be going, you have to be at the pub soon after lunch.'

Gail nodded, 'Yes, mustn't be late on the first day.'

Hugh appeared not to have heard them as he went on slowly,

'Look, will you just listen while I explain, just give me a chance to tell you my side . . . ' he gave a lopsided smile, 'I'm not blaming you . . . ' he looked at Helen for the first time since they had arrived.

'Blaming Mum!' The words erupted from Gail like shots from a gun. 'I should jolly well think not. You're the one to blame, letting her leave here, her home, bringing that . . . that bitch into all our lives. I just don't understand it . . . it's hardly as if you were young and dishy, and she's not much older than I am.'

She turned back to the sink to swill out her mug, having to keep her shaking hands occupied.

For a moment Hugh looked completely devastated as if she had actually struck him, then he said, 'You'll understand one day, how it is . . . '

Gail broke in, 'I hope I never have to, if I thought Alan would go off with some . . . some floozie . . . ' she swallowed hard, unable to finish the sentence.

Hugh looked downcast. 'I know it's difficult for you to appreciate, but people change as they get older . . . you're so young . . . circumstances change.'

Helen got to her feet. 'Honestly Gail I don't think there's much use in pursuing this conversation now.'

Gail swung round, 'It's got to be discussed Mum, you have to know where you stand, it's like some awful nightmare, this lovely cottage, our home.' She gazed round the cottage in its disarray . . . 'Somewhere I always thought would be here forever. It's as though the whole world is crumbling, don't you understand? I feel as if I'm standing in a quicksand, it's even affecting the way I feel about Alan . . . '

Helen put her arm round her shoulders, she could feel her shaking in spite of her valiant efforts to appear in complete control of herself.

'Look darling, it's our problem, your father's and mine. But one thing is certain, it's not going to spoil your happiness, yours and Alan's, it is something we have to sort out for ourselves.' She looked at Hugh over the girl's shoulder, her eyes beseeching.

'Of course you are right. I am sure we can work something out. Anyway it wasn't my idea for your mother to leave here, she suggested she go up to Powdermills. I was quite prepared to move out, to be the one to go.'

'How very generous of you.' Gail sounded sarcastic, completely unlike herself. How sad it was that one person could come into their lives and turn everything sour. Helen could never have imagined Gail speaking to her father like that, as if he were a stranger . . . or she and Hugh referring to each other as 'Your mother, your father,' had it really come to that?

Now she nodded and said, 'That is quite true. It was my suggestion, as a temporary arrangement.' She picked up her handbag. She knew it was useless to try to come to any kind of understanding now. It was as if Hugh had a sickness of some kind which had to burn itself out, a fever in the blood. She had seen it happen so many times to people they knew, but it was like a car accident, a serious illness, death, it always happened to other people, not to your own close, happy family.

8

Hugh opened the car door for Helen, looking from one to the other of them as he said once more, 'Please try to understand . . . ' Neither of them replied. Helen started the car and drove off without a backward glance. For a little while they didn't speak. Then Gail broke the silence,

'What made you pick her for the job out of all the others?'

Helen shrugged her shoulders, keeping her eyes fixed on the road. 'Heaven knows. How do these things happen? Oddly enough I wasn't really all that keen in a way, but her designs were good, different. All the others were so run of the mill, conventional, and at the time she seemed . . . well . . . more mature.'

'She's mature OK,' Gail said bitterly, 'a practised homewrecker.'

Now Helen had to laugh, and it broke the tenseness of the atmosphere.

'How do you know Miss Wisdom? You haven't even been out in the world yet.'

'College is a pretty good microcosm I guess,' the girl replied, 'and one meets people from broken homes all the time, just as I did at school, and not only the couple concerned, but often the other woman or whatever you like to call her. Mostly they seem to be in the same mould, specially when it's someone Dad's age involved.'

Back at Powdermills Gail got her little car out of the shed where she had put it, then she came into the kitchen where Helen was preparing the lunch — a salad, brown rolls, fresh fruit. Gail wrinkled her nose at the smell of the mint sauce she had been making to go with the lamb.

'One of the best smells in the world, fresh mint sauce, and unlike coffee which like other things doesn't live up to its promise, mint sauce does.' She flopped on to a kitchen chair. Helen threw back her head and really laughed for the first time since she could remember.

'That was a highly complicated remark if ever I heard one . . . but I am lucky, someone in the past made a wonderful herb bed just outside the cottage, it only wanted a bit of clearing, and there is everything; fennel, sage, rosemary, mint and even borage if we should be fancying a Pimms Cup!'

'Don't reckon there'll be much demand for those down at the Mermaid on the Barbican,' Gail grinned . . . 'I ought to be there around tea time. Frank Wilson is going to show me the ropes. Actually I worked behind the bar in the club at College so I know a bit about it, it's just the prices that will be different. It's a smashing old pub. You'll have to come and see it. Frank's quite dishy actually . . . ' she paused a moment, 'I've been thinking . . . '

Helen smiled, 'Heaven preserve us! I've had some of your thinking before and like the old saying about the curate's egg, it's good in parts. What now? Not adopting a dog or cat or a bedraggled donkey, good as the causes are, they do create problems.'

'No, nothing like that. There's no accommodation at the pub for me which means Frank says he can find me some digs and the trouble is the chap who owns the pub will only pay half towards them. Now that you're here on your own most of the time would it be possible for me to doss down in one of the bunks to save the lollie on bed and breakfast?'

Helen came over and put her arm round the girl, kissing her on top of the head. Her hair smelt of summer.

'You're a nice kid. Don't know where you get it from, and you don't fool me one bit. You know I'd love to have you, but I don't fancy the idea of you driving back here when the bar closes, and I know it's because you think I need to be kept company.'

'I'm a big girl now and the evenings

are light until late . . . '

'You know I wouldn't be able to say no,' Helen said, 'if you're quite sure. Why don't we give it a trial, see how it works. After all you can sleep later here in the mornings than you'd be able to in digs, and I can see you eat properly . . . as for dossing down in a bunk, what's wrong with the little spare room you used last night?'

'Super, if you don't mind or want it for anyone else.'

'Such as who?'

'Well, two can play at Dad's game . . . you're a very attractive woman if I may say so, and what's sauce for the goose . . . '

Helen frowned a moment, 'That's the last thing I can imagine and it wouldn't improve the situation much would it. In spite of how things may look now I'm still in love with Hugh, and somehow I feel one day, if I can stick it out, he'll come back.' She went on with the preparations for lunch.

'He doesn't deserve you that's all I

can say,' Gail replied, she paused a moment 'and really the old Dad I used to know and love doesn't really deserve that awful girl, so perhaps in the end everything will work out . . . '

Later Helen watched Gail drive off and although she knew this time she would be back in a few hours, she felt bereft after having her company for the last few days. Her mind shied away from the knowledge that before Christmas Gail would be gone to the other side of the world . . . of that she must not think . . . only pray that some miracle would happen in the meantime to bring Hugh back to her . . . 'I must not be a thoughtless, selfish old Mum,' she told herself sternly.

She had gone to bed before Gail returned from Plymouth, but she had lain awake reading, leaving the outside light on, although the afterglow from one of the moor's wonderful sunsets still kept it almost as light as day, the distant tors caught in a noose of gold and crimson reflections. The moor had captured her heart, something good at least that had come out of all the misery. It had brought her solace in one of the most difficult periods of her life. For that she would forever be in its debt . . .

Gail was bursting with life and excitement, although it was after midnight.

'Mum it's really super, you have to come and see it. It goes back to the days of Drake, they say he heard of the approach of the Armada while he was drinking there. Actually I'd never be surprised if the swash-buckling old devil walked in. We get a lot of navy chaps in, and fishermen of course, and lots of grockles . . . by the way do you know where that name for tourists came from?' Not pausing to let Helen reply, she went on, 'It was when they were making a film in the area about the locals conning the holidaymakers and calling them clowns and grockles . . . grockle was from the name Grock, the Swiss clown, a bit before my time but he was apparently a kind of thick comedian. Useless info, but interesting . . . guess I'll cull a lot more in time, could write a book . . . 'Experiences of a Barmaid' — very Jackie Collinsish.' She bent and kissed her mother.

'Sleep well, it's lovely to know you're right next door,' Helen said. Gail turned at the door and blew her mother a kiss, Helen put up her hand and pretended to catch it in flight, as she had done when her daughter was a small girl.

Suddenly, as if a knife were being turned, the pain seared through her chest making her gasp with agony. She clenched her teeth on the sheet so she wouldn't cry out. Whatever happened Gail mustn't know. She lay rigid, the sweat pouring from her . . . at last, after what seemed hours, the spasm decreased leaving her weak, exhausted. Each time now they were taking longer and longer to pass. She knew she had to make an appointment with Gerry Hart, their family doctor who lived in the village. He had known them for years, brought Gail into the world.

Fortunately the next morning Gail was too busy recounting more stories about the customers in the pub to notice the rings under her mother's eyes. Helen had taken her some breakfast in bed and perched on the window seat with her back to the light praying the quick make up she had slapped on would hide her pallor.

She rang the surgery directly Gail had gone that afternoon.

Fortunately Gerry was there and said he would see her at once if she could call in. She had to explain she was living away from home at the moment . . . if he had heard rumours naturally he said nothing, just told her she was lucky to be in such a wonderful spot.

He took her blood pressure, examined her thoroughly, pausing now and then to write down a note, ask about her appetite, how her breathing was normally, about the pain and when it seemed most likely to attack.

'I suppose when I get over-tired . . . or upset,' she hesitated a moment, then said, 'Of course living in the village you must have heard that Hugh and I . . . well we've had a temporary separation.'

He nodded, 'I had heard and it made me sad, but knowing both of you to be sensible people I feel sure you will sort it out, but I think you should tell him you're off colour.'

She shook her head, 'No, that's the last thing I want. I trust you not to say a word either to him or Gail. She is getting married before Christmas.'

He grinned, 'When I hear about the babies I brought into the world now getting married and having their own families it makes me feel my years!'

She grinned back, 'Join the club. It's quite frightening how the time just melts away.'

'Now to return to you, my patient. I am going to give you some tablets to take when the pain occurs. They will help, but they are not a cure. I think it is likely I am being over cautious, but I'd like you to go into hospital — only as an out-patient, for some tests. They'll only take a few hours and the results will put me in the picture.'

Helen nodded, 'Okay, but I still want you to promise absolute secrecy.' He laughed and crossed his throat with one finger, 'I swear absolute silence, my lips are sealed, if that is what you want, but only for the time being,' he added.

She felt reassured as she left the surgery. Obviously there couldn't be much wrong and she knew how these doctors fussed these days and liked to pass you on to the experts for another opinion, even Gerry who was still the old fashioned type of GP, who sat and actually listened to what you had to say. She tucked the little bottle of pills into her bag. How people had come to depend on the universal panacea of the pill, still to many they had brought added years of useful and enjoyable life, so it was not hers to criticise. Perhaps that little bottle would hold the cure she needed, in spite of what Gerry had said.

The next day she drove down with Gail to Plymouth. It was a glorious day of cloudless blue. They parked both cars, for Helen had brought her own as she intended to return before Gail as some students were arriving early in the evening.

It was years since she had visited the Barbican and she was filled afresh with its magic, the cobbled streets and alleyways where once the footfalls of Nelson and other great seafarers sounded. There were antique shops, craft shops, restaurants and cafes with exotic foods from the four corners of the world. They read the names listed on Island House where the Pilgrim Fathers had slept the night before they sailed for America. A warship was moving gracefully through the Sound and fishing boats chugged in with their catches. The old houses up the tiny side streets, some going back more than five hundred years, filled her with a sense of tradition and continuity, which somehow brought comfort in a changing world.

She drove back through the shimmering heat of the moor. As she neared Powdermills along the tarmac track she saw Michael was waiting for her, a piece of paper in his hand.

'An urgent phone call, Mrs Kendall.' He still called her that when he got bothered or upset; when he was sitting quietly eating, or talking normally, she had managed to persuade him to use Helen.

She got out of the car, worried for the moment that something might have happened to Hugh. It couldn't be Gail, she had only just left her safely behind the bar of the Mermaid.

'Doctor Hart . . . could you ring him right away.' He gave her the paper with the number on, 'I took it in case you didn't remember. I knew you had no telephone directory in the cottage.' He gave her a penetrating look, but asked no questions. Michael wouldn't, she thought, then said by way of scotching

118

any ideas he might have, 'It's just about some pills he was getting me, I expect he wants me to call in for the prescription.' She turned to go into the cottage, a thought striking her, 'Oh by the way, although the pills are only for a very minor complaint, you know what Gail's like so don't mention the call to her will you?'

'Of course not if that is what you want.' He turned away and she felt he would have liked her to confide in him.

She went into the cottage and called the number . . . 'Could you come down to the surgery right away Helen? I want to have a talk with you, and I would really rather not do it on the phone.'

She glanced at her watch. There was just time before the students arrived.

'If I must,' she said rather reluctantly, 'but I do have things to do.'

He laughed, 'Oh I realise you're not just a pretty face . . . but I would be glad and it won't take long.'

The receptionist showed her straight in. Gerry got to his feet and pulled out a chair for her, 'Like a coffee?'

She shook her head, 'Thanks, but no. There really isn't time. I do hope this isn't going to take too long.'

He sat down and pulled out a file from the top drawer of his desk. The smile had gone. 'My diagnosis went through to Jack Thorne, he's the heart specialist at Darracombe Hospital.'

She knew it was the new unit in Plymouth which had recently been opened, specialising in heart surgery. For a moment her own heart missed a beat . . . surely it couldn't be as serious as that.

'I think I know you well enough not to pull my punches . . . it is a serious condition you have Helen, something that may have been there when you were born and has only just shown up — time and stress haven't helped. Did you ever have rheumatic fever when you were a kid?'

'Not that I remember. As a matter of fact I was disgustingly healthy. I suppose I had the usual childish complaints of measles, chicken pox, mumps.'

'I see.' He was shuffling the papers obviously finding it difficult to pick the words to say what he had to both simply and plainly. Now he looked straight at her,

'Jack says you need heart surgery — and the sooner the better . . . '

9

Helen was certain she could not have heard right . . . the kind of thing Gerry was talking about was like a serious motor accident, always happening to other people, never yourself. For a moment the thought crossed her mind that she had felt the same about the situation between herself and Hugh . . . that that was not possible. Other marriages broke up because there was another woman. Not one's own. What had happened to her life? Everything was going wrong . . .

Gerry cleared his throat.

'I can't possibly go into hospital at the moment,' she said at last. 'Apart from anything else Gail's wedding has to be arranged, it's only a few weeks off and it isn't as if Alan will be working in England and it can just be postponed. They are going to Australia at the end of November . . . it has to be before that . . . ' As she spoke the thought of all the arrangements she had to make overwhelmed her. She felt the tears start behind her lids. Whatever happened she couldn't give way now. She brushed the tears away, conscious that carefully applied eyeshadow and mascara would be smudged.

She looked up. His eyes were kind, full of compassion making the tears now roll down her cheeks, her voice caught in her throat as she tried to speak.

'Don't you see? It just isn't possible.'

'I hear what you say,' he said slowly, taking off his glasses and swinging them round and round, a habit she had noticed before that he had when something difficult had to be broached.

'Look Helen, I don't know exactly the circumstances of the break up, or separation between you and Hugh, and unless you want to tell me, I don't want to, but you are my patient, your health is all that matters to me, nothing else counts, and this operation, apart from being necessary, will bring you entire relief from pain. Surely it would be easier to face what you have to emotionally, mentally, if at least physically you are without pain.'

She knew what he said made sense. She knew too she was not going to take his advice.

'Surely with a crisis of this sort, at least you can go and talk to Hugh? Damn it, you've been married enough years, Gail is your only child. I think they must be told.'

She stood up. 'Look, I'm very fond of you, we all are, you're the old fashioned type of GP, sadly missing today, I know you mean well and have my interests at heart . . . ' She broke off because he was grinning at her.

'Thanks for the old bit, believe me I feel it, specially when I can't make what I thought was my irresistible charm work on you for your own good.'

She nodded, 'I know, I do know you are thinking of me, but even if it meant . . . ' she hesitated, 'does it? . . . I mean is there a possibility I might collapse, or even worse . . . if I don't have this done right away?'

He looked down and shuffled the papers on his desk. 'To be honest I don't know, no one can know such things with absolute certainty . . . you could go on for months, the pain getting progressively worse, nothing more dramatic than that could happen, as far as onlookers are concerned. I should think for yourself that would be drama enough. On the other hand, given the circumstances all being wrong at the wrong time, if you want it straight, yes, you could collapse, there could be a massive heart failure.'

She sat down again quickly. 'I see. In other words the whole thing rests in my hands, the choice perhaps between life and death. I don't know, somehow I seem to have got so tired of the phrase — 'It's up to you' — so much in my life seems to have been my decision; decisions, decisions . . . '

Once again the glasses swung. 'Perhaps I have made it sound a little too dramatic. There is a remote possibility, yes, but it really is something that not even the best specialist in the land could reassure you on.'

She nodded, 'Yes I know. Only a little while ago a friend of mine had a thorough check up and was passed A 1. She was going on holiday to the Far East and wanted to make sure there was no possibility of anything going wrong. She died in the airport, a massive heart attack, and yet she had been given the all clear . . . so is there any reason the diagnosis couldn't work the other way?'

He shook his head, smiling still. 'No, to be honest, and as you want to talk both yourself and me into postponing the operation I realise there is nothing I can say to persuade you.' He drew his prescription pad towards him, 'so I am going to give you something a little stronger to help you when the pain occurs. You must try to take it easy though, rest as much as you can and directly the wedding is over I put you on your honour to report to me.' He pretended to look at her sternly.

She gave him a mock salute, 'Yes sir . . . ' She took the prescription paper with its hieroglyphics and glancing at it said, 'How in heaven's name any chemist ever reads that kind of thing I'll never know.'

'Just as well not to,' he held out his hand. 'Seriously, Helen, promise to take care, and you know I'm always on the end of the telephone if you need me.'

'Okay, but in exchange you must promise not to tell anyone about this.' She looked at him anxiously 'anyone,' she repeated.

'I give you my word, if that is what you want.'

She drove home slowly. It was so strange, she felt perfectly normal. At the moment there was no pain, no difficulty in breathing, nothing, and yet deep down inside somewhere was this threat, as if some evil spirit dwelt within, waiting to pounce, to threaten. Somehow she had to cope with the knowledge for a few weeks. It was the end of September now, Gail wanted the wedding early in November. She counted on her fingers on the steering wheel . . . four weeks, perhaps five. Surely she could manage to survive that time.

She picked up the pills from the chemist. They looked harmless enough . . . small, white, just like all the other pills that were dished out these days, and yet perhaps they could mean the difference between life and death if the occasion arose.

As she approached Powdermills she thought about Gail. During the weeks she had been working at the Mermaid in some ways she had blossomed out. Perhaps the contact with such widely differing people had done her good. She still refused to see Hugh more than was necessary for the wedding arrangements.

Alan had been down once or twice to

stay for a weekend. The more Helen saw him the more she liked him and thought how right he was for Gail.

Of course he had had to be put in the picture as far as Hugh and Maureen were concerned. His reaction had been both kind and sympathetic, and Helen thought very mature for a young man.

He put his arm round her, 'I do understand how you feel. My parents split up when I was quite a kid,' he hesitated a moment, 'but I can promise you I'll look after Gail, Mrs Kendall.'

'I know you will — and Helen, please, you make me feel about a hundred.'

Also she was thankful that she had had no recurrence of the pain, no need to take the pills. In fact she had almost persuaded herself the doctors were wrong, it was just something that occurred when she got upset. It would pass, resolve itself. In any case whatever else happened, Gail had been upset enough by the situation between herself and Hugh, she certainly was not going to spoil everything now by breaking down and asking her to postpone the wedding.

But sometimes when she lay awake in the early dawn, when her spirits were low and she missed Hugh acutely, she reasoned to herself that she would never tell him, knowing he had a certain sensitivity, or had had, she felt he might well come back to her out of either pity or guilt; that was something she was not prepared to do. As she lay watching the sun come up over the tors in the autumn dawn, she wasn't even sure if she wanted him back now. Powdermills, the moor, her students, even Mike meant so much, had come to mean a lot while she had been there. One thing was certain, she did not want his pity.

October had turned into a real St Martin's summer and a few students still drifted up to Powdermills, attracted largely by the beauty of the moor which was breathtaking. Not a cloud in the blue bowl of sky, the heather stretching away into the shimmering distance, and it was so warm Helen had discarded sweaters and thick slacks for shirts and jeans.

It really seemed as if Powdermills was established as a success and would go ahead with no extra effort on her part. She had set up a demonstration area where she could sit and throw pots on a wheel and people could stand round and watch, she also did hand throwing on a bench which Michael had set up for her. All this seemed to attract people who at first didn't think they wanted to pot themselves, but gradually they became fascinated by the process and wanted to partake. During the height of the summer there had been a tail-back of cars as far as the moorland road.

Michael too was making a big success of his side of the business. Two things seemed to have grabbed people's imagination — metal fire baskets as so many were going back to open grates and demanding chimneys on their houses, and weather vanes. He had made one as an experiment, a mounted

131

rider with a hound at his feet, his whip acting as the pointer. He couldn't keep up with the orders which rolled in, not only for that particular model, but for individual designs. A pub called the Highwayman had ordered such a man for their chimney, there were hounds for hunt kennels, different breeds of dogs for breeders, even a coach with four horses for an old coaching inn. He had actually had to take on part time help.

And then there were the wedding preparations. These were so absorbing that Helen had actually put Hugh and Maureen into the back of her thoughts. So it had been a shock one Sunday when she and Gail had decided to go to one of their favourite places for lunch, an old stables converted into a restaurant, that as they walked in they had passed Hugh and Maureen sitting in intimate proximity in one of the cosy booths.

Helen had been on the point of turning round and leaving, she couldn't face being in the same building. But Gail, immediately aware of the situation, took her hand and led her to the table they had reserved the other end of the dining room. 'Why should they continuously spoil our enjoyment?' she argued.

It was strange how in the past few weeks it was she who had become the strong one.

But Helen's day was spoilt. She didn't really know what she was eating, although Hugh and Maureen were so engrossed in each other they didn't even notice herself and Gail.

She plunged gladly into the wedding preparations, thankful she had Gail for company. Although it was late October, the weather was still like summer, often the three of them — for Michael had become almost one of the family — would take their mid morning coffee outside and sit on the old stone wall, savouring the warmth of the sun, the smells, the sound of the larks who still sang above, and all the beauty the moor had to offer.

'Doubt I could live anywhere else,' Michael said.

Gail grinned, 'Wonder if there's anything to compete with this in the outback.'

Helen thought wistfully, 'If only Hugh were here to enjoy it . . . this would be perfection, but perhaps we are never meant to have such a thing in life.' Then she told herself not to be morbid, she had so much to be thankful for.

The wedding was to be the first Saturday in November. Gail had found a dressmaker on the Barbican, near the Mermaid, who designed and hand sewed the embroidery on the white satin dress, and also made those of her bridesmaids, fellow students whom Helen had offered bunk beds at Powdermills for the weekend. When she had made the suggestion Alan had been staying and he said, 'Great, couldn't be better.' And so it had been arranged.

To their horror, the week before the

wedding nature changed her mind. Overnight the temperature dropped and when Helen and Gail awoke the next morning it was a winter wonderland they saw from their windows. It had snowed in the night, a night which had started full of stars, now there was a brittle coat of ice on the puddles in the road, frost on the grass as bright as the sky, sharpening the voice of the owl who lived in the ruined buildings.

Helen had woken early as always, and this particular morning she saw the grey green dawn heralding the frosty day. There was a flush over the trees in the east, the sun was rising round, and red. Where yesterday the pastures had hissed and gurgled, now as she went down and opened the door and stepped outside, the grass was crisp, no birds sang, except a flock of chaffinches in the hedge opposite the cottage door, who reluctantly left their roosting place when they heard her.

Several of the girls, friends of Gail, were due to arrive the next day. She only hoped there wouldn't be more snow. She went back into the cottage and put on the coffee to percolate, its lovely aroma soon filling the little kitchen. Gail had finished her job last week, quite sorry to leave the pub where she had made many friends and promising to bring her 'cobber' to see them the first time she returned to England. Now she was busy with endless lists, packing, sewing and making endless phone calls, all the preparations of a bride-to-be, with the added complication of going immediately to live abroad.

She and Alan tried not to take sides against Hugh, being as supportive of Helen as they could whilst still remaining tactful, not wishing to exacerbate the situation. It was an uneasy compromise. Hugh came to Powdermills once or twice — something he had avoided before Gail came. He had been quite overwhelmed by the progress Helen had made and the fact that the project was rapidly becoming a major success.

'You're doing better than we are down at the pottery,' he said, looking round at the shelves where the student's work was stacked. Helen had kept meticulous accounts of what she had spent on materials, the fees, and the amounts of cash she had taken for sales of student's work. Hugh tapped his teeth with his pen as he glanced at the neat columns of figures in the books.

'Why didn't we think of doing this before?'

Helen turned away. She thought to herself, we never needed something like this, something that both of us were not involved in . . . together . . .

10

And so once more Helen sat in the little country church, which she hadn't visited since Julie's wedding. This was a very different occasion, from the seasonal point of view apart from everything else; then it had been summer, now it was winter. There had been brightly coloured flowers everywhere filling the church with sunshine, perfume and warmth. Now there were dahlias, lilies, michaelmas daisies and the perfume was of chrysanthemums — sharp, almost Christmassey. But it did look beautiful, and it was still warm and cheerful with candles everywhere, carrying out the theme of scarlet and white.

Hugh had been generous making sure no expense was spared, there was a full choir and he had told Helen to make whatever arrangements she wished for the reception. Once again they had chosen the village pub.

It seemed strange to be sitting next to Hugh in the front pew now his duties were finished. She had a burning desire to put out her hand and touch his, only quenched by the feeling he might reject her. That she could not bear. The service was nearly over. Gail had chosen lovely hymns, 'Praise My Soul the King of Heaven', 'All Things Bright and Beautiful', and the anthem to be played while the register was signed — 'Amazing Grace'. 'I don't really mind if none of it is typically wedding — I want everyone to be happy.' She had squeezed Helen's hand, her eyes beseeching.

She had looked so radiant, Helen had known the tears would stream down her face, but all mothers of the bride were allowed this indulgence, whatever the circumstances. The dress was exactly right, the white satin showing off the slim figure to perfection, a high neck, long sleeves with tiny satin covered buttons, and a full skirt which had been cunningly cut into a train from the back of the waist. Even Hugh had had tears in his eyes when he came to fetch her. She knew he had sent Maureen to London on a sales project and for that at least she was grateful. Several times she had been going to pluck up courage to ask him, for Gail's sake if not hers, to make sure the girl wasn't present, she was thankful at least she had been spared having to ask.

She was thankful too that during the weeks before the wedding, in spite of the fact she had been so busy and sad at the coming parting, at least she had had no return of the pain and was beginning to think perhaps it had been a phase she had gone through. Doctors had been known to be wrong before.

Gail and Alan were not going to have a honeymoon, the wedding night was going to be spent in a very exclusive and expensive London hotel in Park Lane which Hugh had given them as part of their wedding present — the next morning they were catching the plane to Australia from Heathrow.

They had begged Helen to be with them, but she had said no, trying to keep her tone light — 'Come on your honeymoon! You have to be joking . . . God forbid I'm that possessive a Mum, and you know I loathe good byes at airports.' She had turned away, not trusting her voice or her eyes.

Late in the evening she drove back to Powdermills. Hugh too had tried to persuade her to stay at the cottage, rather clumsily explaining Maureen was not expected back for several days, but it held so many memories, both of their marriage and of Gail's childhood that it was more than she could take. Rather desperately, as he saw her to the car, he said, 'We must talk, Helen . . . ' More abruptly than she really intended she said,

'I'm afraid I can't see what about.' And had let in the clutch so sharply that the car had leapt forward in a series of kangaroo hops which nearly brought her to the verge of a kind of hysterical laughter.

The November rain had set in like steel rods, the month now had turned sour as it so often did. There was a bitter north east wind and the sun had set with black clouds over the moor, black hedges lined the colourless fields as she left the foothills. It was impossible to believe there had ever been such a time as summer, that the sun had really shone.

She wondered what Michael was doing. He had been to the wedding but she knew it wasn't really his scene. He hadn't looked particularly comfortable, and although he was polite, she could tell he felt a deep resentment towards Hugh on behalf of herself and Gail. It was an endearing attitude, although probably Hugh had an entirely different angle of resentment then towards his business partner.

Michael had disappeared early. She had rather hoped he might wait and offer to drive her back for she had drunk more champagne than she should, and was always worried in case there should be some kind of accident, even a small bump, and she would be breathalysed and lose her licence, then she really would be in trouble for so much of her livelihood now depended on being able to drive around. That was one thing she was glad about, she was able to support herself and did not have to run to Hugh every five minutes for cash. Although far from being a feminist as such, she could understand how women loved their independence. To be fair perhaps there were one or two things she had to thank Maureen for — that at least, and an added closeness with her daughter, but none of that could compensate for losing Hugh, if that was what it was to come to.

She arrived at Powdermills without mishap, her mouth dry, longing for a cup of tea and feeling weary to the very bones. Michael's old jalopy, as he called it, was parked outside her cottage, not his own. She went through the open front door and found that he had lit the fire in the little sitting room, piling up the logs so that the flames danced and flickered, their reflection bright on the walls, he had lit only the small table lamp. The scene was so cosy it brought a great wave of warmth and comfort to her.

Michael had changed from his suit back into his working clothes, she guessed, with some relief. He had looked rather like a trussed chicken in what was obviously his one and only suit, and the fact that he had put on some weight since he had bought it. The kettle sang on the stove, and he got up from his knees where he had been making toast in front of the fire.

'Michael! How very kind. You shouldn't have gone to all this trouble.'

He grinned lopsidedly looking as endearing as a small child, 'It was only an excuse really. I do hope you won't think me rude but weddings aren't really my thing.' The expression sounded strange on his lips, but she guessed he had picked it up since Gail had been home.

'I can understand that. They are really for women not men.' She flopped down and kicked off her shoes. 'That toast smells marvellous, you'll join me of course.'

He shook his head 'I got a whole pile of unloading to do, a fresh lot of iron just arrived, they left the trailer and will be back for it in the morning. I helped myself to a cup of tea, but it is a fresh pot.'

She would dearly have loved to beg him to stay to keep her company, but realised this new loneliness was something she was going to have to come to terms with, and probably the sooner the better.

The weeks dragged by. There was only a thin sprinkling of visitors and students now, most people were deterred by the idea of getting snowed in on the moor, but it gave her a chance to catch up with working out her plans for the following spring and summer, and she spent a lot of time writing to Gail, who herself was a marvellous letter writer, much to her mother's surprise, and she wrote diary-like letters each week.

'Some parts of Australia are still in the dark ages, the women segregated from the men and really looked upon as some kind of rather superior domestic animal! At dances or socials they still huddle one end of the room while the men, near the drinks naturally, discuss the price of wool, cricket etc. However I am glad to say Alan is not of this ilk! Another strange thing is the layer of snobs, a kind of hierarchy of those who can prove their ancestors came over from choice and not as deportees! It is really quite amusing to watch, fortunately for me Alan's ancestors were among those who chose to come or I should be delegated to the ranks!! Not that I am much bothered, you know me.'

She didn't mention her father and Helen had no idea whether she wrote to him or not. Hugh had suggested Helen come to the cottage for Christmas, but she suspected that Maureen would be there and the idea of being in her own home as some kind of tolerated, patronised visitor was something she could not stomach.

She went down to Widecombe church for the carol service the Sunday before Christmas. It was an amazing experience. The church was packed, people had come from as far away as Somerset and even London, to hear the choir sing, to see the crib. She stood next to a man with the most beautiful voice who sang descant to all the carols. Some of the peace and joy of the festival seeped into her as she listened. Perhaps next year would bring back happiness. At least she knew that Gail and Alan were happy. In her last letter Gail had said, 'You must come out soon, Mum. Never mind about your flying phobia, have a good swig from the scotch bottle before you get on the plane and you'll be here before you know it.' Helen smiled to herself. She did hate the idea of flying. She had only been to Spain once on holiday; the thought of a long trip was daunting, but she could overcome her feelings to see Gail. Although she and Alan hoped to be able to come over to England once a year anyway for a holiday mixed with business. The firm wanted to keep tabs on their Australian branch through him.

It was the day she found the first snowdrops hopefully pushing their silver grey spears through the moss outside her back door that Hugh came to see her. He drove up during the morning. She had been testing the kilns in preparation for the coming season. Although Michael was always ready to help her she felt she must manage on her own. Also lately she had noticed a kind of proprietary manner he had adopted, and sometimes his hand had lain on her shoulder or arm longer than was necessary, his eyes holding a question. The last thing she needed at the moment was any kind of involvement, any complication of his falling in love with her, he was years younger than she, and Hugh's business partner, and Hugh was the man she still loved. He had a letter in his hand as he came into the cottage. She saw the envelope had an Australian stamp but the writing was not Gail's. Her heart missed a beat.

'There's nothing wrong?'

'No, on the contrary. It's from Julie and Brough. Seems they have really gone to town doing market research. There is a big potential in Aussieland, in the big cities, for our kind of thing. At the moment they are pommie orientated as far as ceramics are concerned, seems to be the in thing to buy British pots. And that can't be bad.'

He followed her into the kitchen and gazed round. It was some time since he had been to Powdermills, Michael usually went down to the office to discuss business.

'My goodness, you certainly have made it cosy. You always were a good homemaker.'

She busied herself with the coffee so

he shouldn't see her face. She was not going to let him see how much she needed someone who cared.

Maybe he was starting to tire, maybe things with Maureen were not developing quite as he had hoped. A small flame of hope started up inside her. She poured the coffee, added cream and sugar as he liked it. He spread out the airmail sheets on the table.

'Brough of course has friends and relatives all over Australia, the prospects are so good that he suggests we come over,' he hesitated a moment, 'How do you feel about it?'

The chance of going to Australia, of seeing Gail was wonderful. As if he guessed her reaction he said quickly,

'I'm afraid there wouldn't be much time to spend with the kids, it would be a kind of whistle stop tour, rushing from one city to another, mostly by plane, living out of a suitcase.'

'I . . . ' she hesitated, half wondering now if she should tell him about her heart condition. She knew Gerry would probably be very reluctant for her to go on such a long and trying trip and she would have to tell him, it would only be fair. She glanced round the room.

'I do have a lot of commitments. I was hoping to go and stay with Gail later in the year, she had asked me, that would be much nicer than just a flying visit, a couple of days and I must admit the idea of all that travelling doesn't appeal . . . you know about me and planes.'

He was folding the letter and putting it back in his pocket. 'I understand. I think perhaps you are wise, so leave it to me. I'll take care of it. Perhaps in the meantime you could pop down to the pottery now and then, keep an eye on things.' He gave her a level glance. Did that mean he didn't trust Maureen? She longed to ask but pride prevented her.

He finished his coffee and stood up. 'I must be off. Lots of things to do. I'll give you a bell before I leave, might be quite soon if I can get a flight.' He kissed her briefly on the cheek. To her surprise she felt nothing. It had been the kind of kiss you give a child as a reward, a reward for what?

When he had gone she felt full of doubts. Perhaps she should have said she would make the trip, but actually if she thought about it she had lost touch with the current situation at the pottery anyway. It was ages since she had been down there, she had become so wrapped up in Powdermills, anyway now she had built up a reputation and a clientele it seemed foolish to throw it all away by being absent, even with the chance of seeing Gail, and anyway she would be seeing her later in the year.

It was only ten days later that Hugh rang to say it was all arranged. If he had time he'd call in on Gail and Alan, but he hadn't been in touch in case it didn't come off and she might be disappointed. For a moment Helen felt an intense loneliness. All the people closest to her were half a world away, but she said 'Best of luck. Hope you come back with a huge stack of orders.'

For the next few days she kept busy and suddenly she realised Hugh had been gone for a week and she hadn't done as he asked, and visited the pottery.

She drove down to the village wondering if she should call at the cottage and see if Mrs Riley was keeping the place clean, but the thought that she might run into Maureen deterred her. However as she passed the door opened and Mrs Riley emerged. Helen drew into the kerb.

'I'm just going down to the pottery. Is everything okay?'

Mrs Riley nodded, 'Yes M'am, I light the boiler twice a week to keep things aired now they've gone.'

'They?' Had she heard right, it must be a slip of the tongue. The woman gave her a curious look.

'The master and that Miss Maureen, left over a week ago.'

Helen thought she would pass out . . . so that was it. All along he had intended to take Maureen, far from things being less sure between them how wrong she had been. She turned the car and drove back to Powdermills. She couldn't face the workers, the office staff at the pottery. She felt the first twinges of pain starting up and realised she had left her pills on the kitchen table.

For a moment she didn't care, didn't care if she lived or died, there was nothing left to live for anyway, without Hugh.

11

Somehow Helen managed to negotiate the narrow moorland roads back to Powdermills, the pain like some wild creature with claws tearing inside her. She had shaken out the contents of her handbag on the car seat, hoping she was wrong and she had the bottle of pills with her, but she remembered now, she had meant to pick them up and take them just in case. Somehow the knowledge that she had them with her worked like a kind of insurance against the pain attacking, but her mind had been in such a state of confusion since Hugh had left for Australia, she knew she was becoming forgetful, and now with this new shock.

There was no sign of Mike, for which she was thankful, although she was nearly passing out with the pain, she knew he would fuss, there would have to be explanations and at the moment she simply felt unable to cope with such a situation.

She threw herself down into the nearest chair when she reached the kitchen, shook out two of the pills and gulped them down with the dregs of the coffee left in the mug. How long she sat there she didn't know, unsure if she actually lost consciousness. She could hear the distant sounds of Mike working in the forge now. She was thankful she was expecting no one for the rest of the day. But she was not going to be able to go on like this. She would have to go into hospital as Gerry had suggested. But when, how, just when the Powdermills prospect was really on its feet, and she had found some kind of consolation in independence . . . but had she really? She dropped her head on her hands and despair once more flooded through her. The only thought that kept her going at all was the knowledge that later in the year she would be going out to see Gail, although in some ways that would produce fresh problems. Somehow she would have to find someone who could keep an eye on the pottery. The student side would have to close for a month. Life seemed to be just one long series of problems.

At last the pills were starting to work. Gradually the pain receded leaving her feeling wrung out like a rag, totally drained. Slowly she got to her feet, weak and shaky from the intensity of the agony.

She boiled an egg and made some coffee and toast. The thought of food made her feel quite sick, but she had to keep up her strength.

She had just finished when the phone rang. For a moment she was tempted to let it ring, but there was something about the urgent insistence of its bell which she could not ignore. She knew some people could cheerfully leave it to ring, or take it off the hook, but always her mind questioned whether it might be someone in trouble, or someone she loved who needed her.

She lifted the receiver. She recognised Hugh's secretary's voice at once. Guilt swept over her. Because of her own private misery she hadn't been into the pottery after all. It was part of her duty and she had neglected it. Whatever her feelings about Hugh and Maureen the business was still partly hers.

'I'm so sorry I haven't been down, Kaye.'

The girl broke in, 'Oh that's all right Mrs Kendall. I know how busy you are up at Powdermills, but something has come up.'

'Nothing wrong, no bad news or anything?'

'Oh no, in fact it could be good news. A man called in yesterday asking to see Mr Kendall. I told him he was abroad so he asked for you. Actually I couldn't get hold of you at the time, there was no reply on the phone. His name is Rowland, Geoffrey Rowland. It seems he is the chairman of Bellams.' She paused a moment as if to let the portent of this information sink in.

'Bellams?' Although the name was familiar, for the moment Helen couldn't connect it with anything.

'Yes, the big firm from Stoke-on-Trent, they make holiday souvenirs, that kind of thing.'

'Of course.' Helen gathered her scattered wits. 'Well what did he want with us? He's hardly in the same league as Kendalls, although of course it is a much bigger concern.'

'He didn't say, said he would only talk to the management. He did leave some notes, they're on your desk.' Kaye sounded a little miffed. She had been with Hugh for many years, and was his trusted confidante, middle aged, a spinster with an invalid mother to keep, entirely trustworthy and reliable if rather dull. A trait which certainly didn't matter as her business acumen and handling of customers and suppliers in tricky situations worked like magic.

'I see. Have you made an appointment for me to meet him?'

'Yes. I made a tentative arrangement for lunch tomorrow. I do hope I did right Mrs Kendall. It did seem rather urgent.'

'Of course, you did quite right. I'll be at the pottery about twelve. Would you make sure the drinks cupboard is stocked?'

'Oh it is.' Kaye sounded slightly reproving now.

Helen had to give a little smile of satisfaction. She knew Kaye didn't like Maureen. She was anathema to her rather prim, sheltered way of life.

Helen put the phone down and sat for a moment without moving. Ideas, thoughts coursing through her mind. The first thing that occurred to her was that he had come to make some kind of takeover bid, they were much in fashion at the moment in both big and small businesses. She couldn't imagine anything much less could have brought such a man as him down to a rather remote pottery in Devon. And yet she couldn't imagine Kendalls could be worth his consideration, or their products. However, it was no good speculating. What she needed was a good night's sleep. Somehow she must be on good form in Hugh's absence.

It was strange, whatever she might feel about him, about Maureen, still the involvement, the interest, the love for the work which they had done together for so many years, counted for something, held her in thrall. That part of her past was something no one could take from her.

She washed her hair. It needed a perm, but she set it carefully on rollers and gave herself a face pack Gail had left behind, while it dried. Why on earth was she taking so much trouble? Was it because she felt she needed to make an impression on this man? Or was it a kind of defiance, a self assurance that she could still deal with the business side of things as efficiently as ever, in spite of what might be going on in her private life.

Before she went to bed she sat down

and wrote a long letter to Gail. She wrote every week in diary form, trying to keep her tone light and amusing. Gail replied in the same way, she was busy with decorating and furnishing the flat the firm had provided, and doing a part time job although Alan had insisted it was quite unnecessary.

'Somehow I don't see myself as a lady of leisure,' she had written. But she sounded cheerful and happy and Helen was relieved she had settled down.

Much to her surprise she had a good night's sleep and woke refreshed, every trace of the pain had vanished, making her as always, convinced the doctors had been wrong, they were known to make mistakes, perhaps it was just something that occurred as a result of nervous tension. It would go away if she made up her mind.

It was a beautiful day, clear blue sky, some early morning frost still lingered like sparkling diamonds in the hollows where the sun hadn't reached, but the roads were dry and already she could imagine she smelt spring on the moorland air among the gorse and bracken. She turned on the radio and sang along with the music as she drove. Why this change of mood? Why was she so cheerful? She had no idea. Perhaps she had come to terms with life to some extent. Someone had once said the more things change the more they are the same. Anyway it was best to count your blessings and she still had many.

A few minutes after she arrived at the pottery a big cream Merc drew up in the car park. She looked down from Hugh's office on the first floor. A man got out of the driving seat. Someone sat in the passenger seat. It looked as if he wore a chauffeur's uniform with a peaked cap. Strange to have a chauffeur and drive yourself! Perhaps this Geoffrey Rowland was unusual.

Kaye brought him to the door. Helen was sitting at the desk, a pile of files and correspondence in front of her, none of which she had actually read, but she was determined to put up a front of involvement and efficiency.

She was totally unprepared for the man who stood in the doorway. She caught her breath.

Then she had a purely childish desire to giggle for he was so like Paul Newman, the film star it was as if his double stood before her. Had he deliberately fostered the look, the obvious likeness she wondered. He must be aware of it, hundreds of people, apart from his own mirror must have told him so. The only difference was that in the last picture she had seen of Paul Newman his hair had turned grey, whereas Geoff Rowland's was still as golden as corn. The intensely blue eyes, crinkled at the corners, regarded her. She wasn't sure if they held amusement or simply assessment. She had the immediate feeling that the facade of files and letters had fooled him not one iota.

She stood up as he came into the room, his hand outstretched, taking hers in a firm grip. The dark grey suit was fitted to the broad shoulders and slim waist and hips as if it had been moulded to him. He wore a brilliant white shirt and gold cuff links caught the sunlight. Suddenly she felt nervous, unsure. Oh God, she prayed, please don't let the pain start.

She indicated the chair opposite her. 'Please sit down. Would you prefer coffee or a drink?'

'Coffee please.' He had a melodious, classless voice. The kind she had once heard described as mid-Atlantic.

'Very wise,' she said, lifting the phone and asking Kaye to bring two cups of coffee. She felt flustered, she had meant to be calm, detached, she babbled on to cover her confusion. 'The trouble with the breathalyser one can never tell if one is over the top, and as far as I'm concerned to lose my driving licence would be a real problem.'

His eyes were quizzical as he looked back at her. 'That is exactly why I take a driver with me. It's worth every penny of his salary. Usually I drive myself, he is there as an added insurance.'

He opened the black despatch case and brought out a pile of neat files which he spread out revealing computer sheets neatly clipped together. He ran his finger down some columns of figures and then said slowly,

'Kendalls have been fluctuating in their fortunes a little lately haven't they Mrs Kendall?'

For a moment Helen was filled with an unreasoning anger at this outsider, this stranger making such a remark.

'Mr Rowland you haven't even told me your business yet — before you criticise Kendalls perhaps you would tell me if you are here to sell, to buy or simply to give me a run down or print out, or whatever you like to call it on our financial position.'

He shut the file and put out his hand, palm upwards. 'Mrs Kendall, I do apologise. I thought your secretary had probably filled you in. I did give her some quick comprehensive notes.' For a moment his eyes flicked over the closed files. Then he pulled a catalogue from the case and laid it in front of her. 'Those are our main lines — holiday souvenirs, mostly quite cheap china, we are hardly as classy as you, but,' he paused and grinned disarmingly 'we do have a pretty healthy turnover.'

Helen felt like replying 'Lucky old you,' but she said, 'Yes Mr Rowland. So?'

He had the grace to look slightly abashed. 'Well I thought perhaps we could come to some arrangement. I realise that these days people want more than just a mug with A PRESENT FROM DARTMOOR PRISON or some slightly rude inscription. Many are interested in genuine collectors items, there are things like ceramic thimble sets, birds, flowers, figurines. Although Rowlands products are of reasonable quality, we would like to have an up-market side to the business.'

'I can see that but I still don't quite understand your intentions in all this, and I thought the firm was called Bellams.'

He looked down at his hands for a moment, then lifted his eyes, 'How about lunch? I find it so much easier to discuss business in a relaxed atmosphere, the working lunch, there is something rather cold, stark and impersonal about offices, however nice, don't you agree?'

Helen nodded. 'Of course. We have a very good pub in the village, they do a first class lunch. I should be delighted to take you there.'

He smiled and shook his head. 'I hope the age of chivalry is not totally dead. Please I insist on your being my guest.'

Geoff Rowland was an accomplished and charming host. He handed her the menu, 'I shall leave the choice entirely to you, Mrs Kendall, you know your local dishes best.'

Helen felt really hungry for the first time for months, she had had only a cup of coffee before she came out. As this man was obviously so rich and successful she was tempted to choose the most expensive dishes listed. Today they were smoked salmon, pheasant, lobster thermidor — for although the pub might be in the centre of a small village, Joan and Sam were professional caterers, and their fame had spread far and wide so that people came from all over the county to eat.

'Excellent taste. I shall follow suit,' he grinned at her, his teeth white and even. She guessed he must be in his late thirties or early forties, but he still had the figure of a younger man. His hands were strong and yet artistic with long, tapering fingers. She wondered if he was artistic and did some of the designing for Bellams.

Once again it was almost as if he were reading her mind. 'Pity you lost your designer, Mrs Kendall.'

He had taken her by surprise, thrown her off balance. She felt a little ruffle of annoyance, hesitating before she said, 'You seem to be exceptionally well briefed on Kendalls, Mr Rowland.'

He grinned disarmingly, pouring the

wine he had ordered, a white burgundy which was one of Helen's favourites. Had this man second sight?

'I know,' he sipped his wine slowly, savouring it, rolling it round his mouth. 'Excellent, remarkably good. Obviously these people know their business. Now we are in a nice relaxed atmosphere, I can tell you what my visit is all about. As you probably know, Bellams, which, incidentally is now Rowlands, none of the original family are left, the firm is run by a board of governors of which I am Chairman. I won't bore you at the moment with the actual hierarchy, in the past we had a reputation mostly for holiday souvenirs, in fact the firm has been going long enough once to have been involved in the making of crested china, now becoming collectors pieces. In its heyday of course it was a cheap form of souvenir, we have remained much in this category, we are not exactly as classy or up market as yourselves, if you will forgive the comparison.' He looked at her quizzically, one eyebrow lifted, 'but at least the china itself is of reasonable quality.'

He was interrupted by the arrival of the smoked salmon, accompanied by wafer thin brown bread and butter, quarters of lemon and a china container of black pepper — one of Kendall's she was amused to notice. All his actions were meticulous without being fussy, as if he enjoyed the actual quality of the things he touched, feeling the shapes, the textures of the lemon, the pepper pot. Helen watched him, fascinated, until she realised his eyes were on her and she dropped her gaze, feeling the warm blood tinge her cheeks red.

'As a matter of fact at one time I did quite a lot of the designing myself. I was a student at both Slade and the Sorbonne, but the business side started to fascinate me, particularly the world of computers and electronics. I find that world intriguing. However, that is beside the point. Just before last Christmas I had an idea, amongst others, to produce a number of different sized good quality ceramic bowls, then to get one of the top chefs to make a really exotic Christmas pudding, perhaps along the lines of the best of Mrs Beaton, traditional rich, and then combining the two for up market sales to the top stores. Each basin would be of individual design, able to stand boiling water with the pudding still inside of course, and then these could become collectors pieces. There could be a range from say a half-pound size up to three or four.' He paused and looked at her, twirling his wine glass in his fingers.

Actually Helen thought it quite brilliant, the designs for the different bowls would be a fascinating challenge, they could range through the seasons, or have flower motifs, or even be taken from old prints. Her mind started to work on the idea at once. She looked at him with shining eyes.

'I think it's fantastic!'

To her surprise he threw back his head and roared with laughter. 'You sound like a charming schoolgirl — honestly I can't go on calling you Mrs Kendall.'

'Of course not, Helen, please.'

'A lovely name for a beautiful woman. The face that launched a thousand ships.'

Once more she felt herself go scarlet. It was ages since she had blushed like some silly sentimental teenager. Neither could she remember having enjoyed herself so much for years. For a moment she felt a stab of guilt as she thought of Hugh — then she remembered how Maureen had behaved when she and Gail had gone to their cottage. Why not take what pleasure she could? Anyway she was doing no one any harm.

'Let me come to the final point,' he was going on, 'but just before I do, would you like another bottle of wine or perhaps a brandy?'

Helen shook her head vigorously. She was already feeling quite lightheaded, but whether it was the presence of this remarkable man, or the wine, or a combination of both she wasn't sure.

'Thanks, but no thanks. I haven't been drinking much lately,' she broke off laughing: 'that sounds terrible, as though normally I'm an alcoholic, but what I mean is since I've been alone . . . since my husband has been away on business, and I have to rely on myself to drive, I have to be careful.'

'Of course. In any case I myself dislike drinking too much at lunch time, the evening is far better when one can relax.' He hesitated as if he were about to add something then changed his mind.

'Back to business. I would like your firm to design the bowls of course, but that is not all. As I told you earlier, I do realise things have not been going too well for Kendalls lately. I feel that perhaps an injection of cash would be welcome. In fact the real purpose

174

behind my visit is to ask if you feel like selling out to Bellams, lock stock and barrel, or, alternatively to come to some arrangement for yourself and your husband to remain as directors.'

Helen felt as if the breath had been knocked out of her, although in some ways she had half expected something of the sort, the reality was a shock. For a moment anger was her chief emotion — anger at his rather calm assumption — albeit an accurate assessment of the situation.

Her eyes blazed now as she looked straight at him. 'Certainly not! What on earth gave you that idea? All firms have their ups and downs, purple patches if you like, and we are just going, or have gone, through one. But there are lots of new ideas in the pipe line. New designs — and of course my husband Hugh is on a tour of Australia. He is sure to return with a full order book.'

Her words left him entirely unruffled. He just smiled . . . 'I know of course that any business is never plain sailing, and at the moment everyone, everything is in the melting pot, but fortunately china is one thing I think people will always need and like, good china and porcelain have an aesthetic quality, certainly the Kendall products have.'

'Flattery will get you nowhere,' she said shortly. She had the feeling again that he knew all about not only the business side of Kendalls, but the domestic problems too.

'Look Helen, I'm a self made man as you probably realise. I started at Bellams firing the kilns, sweeping the floors, fetching and carrying. I'm not ashamed of my humble beginnings. My family scraped and saved to send me to Art School, I won scholarships, none of it was easy. I know what building up your business must have been like, the toll such things take. But there comes a time when one must be ruthless, that is a hard lesson I had to learn myself.'

Helen could appreciate this. Under the charm she realised there was a streak of dynamism, detached business acumen. She admired him for admitting it. But she shook her head. 'I really have to assure you that the business is not for sale on any terms and I am confident that my husband would back me to the hilt in saying this.'

'I am not really surprised by your answer, but at least it was worth a try.' He called for the bill, his tone and expression totally disarming, 'but I would very much like to look round the pottery if I may and perhaps have some further discussions on the idea of the bowls, which I hope you will agree to collaborate on. I know it is early in the year, but as you of all people will appreciate, these ideas take time to formulate.'

She nodded, 'Yes, I like the idea very much as a matter of fact. I think there is no doubt we could come to some agreement over it, and I should like to submit some design ideas myself. It has great appeal.'

'Great, to celebrate will you dine with me tomorrow night? I have business to do in Plymouth and Exeter, but I shall be finished by six at the latest. Perhaps we could combine dinner with dancing. I am staying at the Royal in Tormouth, and I noticed they have a dinner dance tomorrow night.'

Helen was too taken aback to speak for a moment. She got to her feet, 'I . . . '

He grinned. 'Oh come on. All work and no play, you know.'

Her mind was going through her wardrobe. She had nothing she could wear to a place like the Royal. It was a five star hotel, known all over the world for its excellence. Royalty, the top stars of films and tv stayed there.

'I know. You've nothing to wear.' He grinned like a triumphant small boy.

'As a matter of fact you're right.'

'Well then, with the thought of the big order Kendalls are going to get from Rowlands, why not treat yourself to a new dress? I'm sure your husband would approve.'

She smiled back. 'I'll do just that. But

if you have time before you go back north, there is something I would like to show you. Powdermills, I don't think that is entered on your computer files. In a way it's nothing to do with Kendalls, it's my own particular baby, something that came out of the blue and has turned out to be a success. At the moment it is not really considered part of the main pottery business.'

'I'd like that.'

She noticed that he didn't say whether he already knew about Powdermills or not. He glanced at his watch.

'I haven't got a meeting until four o'clock. How about showing me round now? We can take my car and I'll drop you back here later so you don't have to drive yourself.'

She was about to protest that she would take her own car, but remembered that she had drunk some wine. She realised he was being tactful, thoughtful.

As they drew up at Powdermills she

was glad to see Mike's car was missing. She wasn't quite sure why. Somehow she felt he would not approve of Geoff . . . they were about as alike as chalk and cheese.

He was charmed and fascinated by Powdermills and the whole conception, as she had known he would be.

He picked up the figurines and pots the students had made.

'Some of these are quite brilliant. I must say I never cease to be amazed at the talent there is, and you must get immense pleasure fostering this.'

The idea of people being able to watch her at work at the wheel appealed to him too. Without realising that he did so, he picked out many of her own designs for admiration, turning them round in his slim fingers, placing them on a shelf of their own.

'Whoever designed these is an expert — original — exactly what I am looking for in these bowls.'

She laughed and gave a mock bow. 'Thank you kind sir, they are my own humble offerings.'

'There is nothing humble about these, or this place.' He looked round approvingly. 'A marvellous conception combining a kind of holiday atmosphere with creative accomplishment and potting.'

'I am fully booked up these days and have little trouble in selling most of the students' work too.'

He sat down at the kitchen table, looking somehow at home and yet alien, which was part of his charm. He was an enigma. She wondered if he was married and yet why should she be interested? She was married herself.

He glanced at his watch. 'I must go. I'll drop you back at the pub to pick up your car. Will that be okay?'

'Of course.'

For some reason she was glad the cream Merc had left Powdermills before Mike returned. She felt guilty. It was ridiculous. Why should she?

When Geoff had dropped her off to pick up her own car she drove into

Tormouth. There was a small dress shop there selling models, dresses and suits. They were wildly expensive but she felt a sense of adventure, of freedom. She wanted something really expensive, exotic, luxurious.

The girl produced half a dozen dresses, all of which Helen fell in love with. But the one she chose was black panne velvet, very fashionable material this season so she was told. It was strapless but had its own chiffon shawl. The skirt was full, ankle length and there was a huge taffeta bow which tied at the back. As she regarded her reflection in the long mirror she couldn't help but be pleased with the result. She felt like a teenager on her first date.

Geoff had promised to pick her up from Powdermills at seven thirty. It was seven o'clock when a delivery van drew up. She had just had her bath and was in her dressing gown. She wondered what on earth they could want, she wasn't expecting any deliveries. The driver handed her a small plastic box. Inside was an exquisite orchid and a small white envelope was attached. She opened it and read 'To a beautiful woman, anticipating a wonderful evening. Forgive me for being so presumptuous as to attempt to gild the lily. With love, Geoff.'

She stood with it in her hand. It couldn't be possible, she had never looked at anyone, never thought of anyone but Hugh, now those blue eyes, that smile, the memory of those hands with their tapering fingers filled her mind.

He had revived her flagging ego, made her aware of herself as a woman again. Could there be any harm in that? Her heart told her no. She did not listen to her head.

12

It was one of the most wonderful evenings Helen could remember. They dined in a room which had one whole wall of glass looking out over the sea where the sun had set, leaving a crimson and orange afterglow, paling to primrose and turquoise where the moon and one bright star hung.

The hotel was so close to the sea that it was like being on board ship, being early in the year there were only a few people at the other tables, most of them were in evening dress which probably meant they were going on to the dance which was to be held in the very exclusive club which had been made in what had once been the wine cellars, and of which residents automatically became temporary members.

The food was luxurious in the extreme and the service smooth and unobtrusive. It was lovely to be pampered, spoiled, considered. A bottle of champagne stood in a silver ice bucket at Geoff's side. He lifted his glass, the bubbles dancing and sparkling in the light of the scarlet candles in their silver candelabra on the table.

'What shall we drink to, Helen? To us, to Kendalls and Rowlands or just to the night?'

For a moment she was tempted to say 'To us!' and to forget all the problems, the difficulties, the sadness. How easy it would be to. She looked up and saw his eyes in their azure brilliance. She wasn't sure what she read in them, this man was an enigma.

'Oh to Kendalls and Rowlands of course!' Somehow her voice sounded school-marmish, but if he was rebuffed, or if he even noticed she was not sure.

He took her hand in his and said, 'Of course. Your husband is a fortunate man, to have a beautiful wife who is both business and life partner, and with such success it is indeed a gift from the gods.'

He sounded more serious than she had heard him yet in their brief friendship, but it was his words more than his tone which suddenly pulled her up and affected her deeply. She *was* lucky, even now with the business with Maureen. She and Hugh had had many years of life and love, of mutual interest in their business — and Gail, who had been a result of that love. She had had so much more than many people. Had she been over emphasising this business with the girl, letting her imagination run riot even perhaps as a result of not being well, although she was reluctant to acknowledge that possibility. Could it be she had even been a little unfair walking out on Hugh, starting up a separate business, having other interests. After all at the marriage service she had promised for better or worse, in sickness and in health. Maybe this was a kind of sickness which she must see him through, something that would pass if she gave him her love and support, understanding. Maybe as Shakespeare had said in Julius Caesar — 'The fault lies not in our stars but in ourselves . . . ' Had it taken this attractive man, this man who, in Gail's parlance, she could have 'fancied', to bring her to her senses? His admiration was obvious, but his envy too for she had caught a hint of that in his tone.

She felt he was watching her. She lifted her eyes and looked him full in the face.

'You know, I *am* lucky, and it does one good to be reminded of it sometimes. We are easily lulled into taking things for granted, becoming ungrateful.'

He grinned, 'I'm sure you never do.' But she guessed he knew he had touched a chord somewhere.

He emptied the bottle of wine into their glasses. Drinking his down he said, 'Shall we dance?'

They went down the shallow stairs which led to the Commodore Club.

There was a gaming room where you could play cards, roulette, *chemin de fer*, or whatever took your fancy. Beyond was a bar and the small ballroom, the lights were dim, the music soft and dreamy. It was lovely to be swept back in time, away from the ubiquitous disco, the too loud, tuneless music which seemed to permeate everywhere these days.

Gosh I'm getting old, Helen thought with a wry smile, what on earth would Gail say to me.

Geoff was a wonderful dancer, as she knew he would be. She had thought as it was so long since she had danced she would be clumsy and unsure.

'I can't remember when I last danced a waltz,' she said tentatively as he swept her up to the lilting music. He held her close so that she fitted into the firm contours of his body, and somehow her feet found no difficulty in following his every movement.

As the music stopped he led her back

to the small table on the edge of the dance floor.

'If that performance is not being able to dance, as you said, then I'm glad you didn't tell me you were a first class exponent or I should have been too nervous even to attempt to partner you!'

She threw back her head and laughed, 'You really are the smooth one. You should be a member of parliament or a diplomat.'

'Good. Then we'll try a tango and then a samba. I'm going to give you the full treatment, you have a wonderful sense of rhythm and that is what dancing is all about.'

Helen felt no tiredness as she had feared she might, in fact it was elation that filled her, due partly to the atmosphere, the music, the wine, and this man, but she also felt a serenity concerning Hugh that she hadn't known for months. Now she longed for him to return, to be able to pick up the pieces, to come to terms with the situation. It was really most extraordinary that this should be the outcome of the evening — the last thing she had expected . . .

All too soon it was over, it was the last dance, the last drink.

'I feel like Cinderella when the ball was over,' she said as they made their way to the car which the chauffeur had brought to the door. She hesitated before she got in.

'You know honestly I could get a taxi. It seems ridiculous to drag you right out to Powdermills at this time of the night, or rather morning.'

He grinned, 'You wouldn't spoil my evening, begrudge me a drive through the moonlight with a beautiful woman.' Gently he pushed her into the back seat and followed her. The car moved swiftly and smoothly away from the lights of the hotel.

It was almost as if Geoff had sensed all the emotions, the feelings which had been chasing through her mind for much to her surprise he now became again the business tycoon rather than just a charming escort for the evening.

'I shall be sending through details and a specimen contract for the ideas we discussed for the Christmas market, and perhaps when your husband returns you'd tell him the different suggestions and let me know his views.'

'Of course.' She gazed out across the moor — stark, mysterious but beautiful as ever in the silver light of the moon. She smiled to herself, wondering what Gail would think when she told her about her 'date' — probably now she was becoming a native 'Oz', as she described Australia — her expression would be 'Good on you, Mum.'

She couldn't resist turning back to Geoff and laying her hand lightly on his. She felt his fingers curl round hers for the moment in a firm grasp. 'I know it sounds nosey, but we have had a wonderful evening, and yet you haven't told me a thing about yourself, apart from the business point of view.' He withdrew his hand and she wondered if she had made a mistake, gone too far and invaded his privacy. She could see his profile silhouetted against the moonlight beyond the car window.

But his voice was still gentle as he said, 'It's not a particularly interesting or pretty story,' she sensed rather than saw him shrug his shoulders. 'In a way one of those 'What-might-have-been' tales. Jose, my wife, was Spanish, a strict Catholic, and very much part of her big family. I don't honestly know why she married me because I don't think she had any intention of living in England, and she knew I had to for my livelihood. We had two children in rapid succession. She was very ill on both occasions. When I had protested after the first one that we have no more, with her Catholic upbringing she was shocked, hurt, and somehow that started the trouble between us. Anyway in the end we agreed to part, to call it a day, it was all pretty messy and painful. She went back to her family in Madrid.'

'And the children?' Helen felt near to

tears at the poignancy of the story, of the innate loneliness of this man.

'Jose took them. I am allowed what they call 'Access' twice a year, but really we are strangers. They hardly speak any English.'

'I am so sorry.' How inadequate it sounded for what she felt.

He turned to her, smiling, she could see the whiteness of his teeth in the moonlight. '*C'est la vie*,' he replied lightly, 'and at least I have a clear conscience in enjoying the company of delightful ladies such as yourself.' He lifted her hand to his lips and kissed her finger tips. 'When they are happily married, then I just have to content myself, as I said, with the phrase 'What-might-have-been' — those words and 'If only', perhaps the saddest in the English language, but I have many compensations. I love my work, I enjoy music, sport, good food and wine, and I am lucky that I can afford to indulge all these tastes. Believe me, I am not at all sorry for myself.'

193

They had reached Powdermills. She felt sure the chauffeur must wonder where on earth his boss had directed him, it probably seemed like the end of the world to a city bred man. He got out and opened the door for Helen. She turned, leaning forward into the interior of the car.

'Will you come in for a cup of coffee, or even something stronger?'

He shook his head, 'Thanks, but no. I have an early start in the morning.' He drew her towards him for a moment and kissed her full on the lips, an electric shock ran along her nerves. Gently he pushed her from him and shut the car door. She stood watching the twin ruby lights disappear giving a deep sigh, her fingers on her mouth where he had kissed her. The words 'What might have been,' lingered for a moment on the fringe of her mind ... it was some hours before she managed to sleep.

13

Helen was making her breakfast coffee the next morning when the phone rang. Who on earth could be ringing at such an early hour, for the sun had woken her, the warmth on her face bringing a real promise of spring? She had been unable to lie in bed any longer.

As she lifted the receiver Hugh's voice came over the line so clearly she thought he must have arrived in England without her knowing.

'How are you? Where are you?' she asked breathlessly.

'Fair dinkum is the answer to the first question, and in Melbourne to the second.' He sounded like his old self, all the tiredness and staleness gone from his voice. 'I'm on my way home, thought I'd just let you know. I've done some wonderful business. Seen Julie and Brough. Actually we've set up an agency which Julie is going to run. There's a terrific demand for pommie products at the moment, we are ace high as they say. Don't really know why. Could be to do with that visit of Di and Charles way back. Anyway we're really in fashion. Gail and Alan are fine too, send all their love and are looking forward to seeing you soon.' He paused for breath and Helen said,

'You haven't been overdoing it?'

'Not on your life. Never been fitter. This is a wonderful country, but they're good at driving a bargain, however, once made they keep their word. I'll be home in a couple of days, give you all the gen then.'

'Shall I meet you at Heathrow?'

'No, it's too much of a hassle. It's easy enough on the train and I haven't much luggage, except the load of orders in my briefcase of course.'

It was wonderful to hear him so cheerful, so like the old Hugh, 'Can't wait to get home I must say, you're okay love?'

She paused a moment to draw breath, keeping her fingers crossed, 'Yes, yes I'm fine. Been fairly busy too, got a bit of news. Hope you'll think it good, not quite up to your standard though.'

'Could you manage to be at the cottage do you think?'

'At the cottage?' She wasn't sure if she had heard right. Did that mean Maureen wasn't with him? Surely he wouldn't ask her if the two of them were returning, he wouldn't be so cruel. There had been no mention of her name. A little spurt of joy started up somewhere deep down inside, a glimmer of hope. 'Of course I'll be there, if you ring me from the airport I'll have a meal ready.'

She stood for a long time after he'd rung off, staring down at the telephone. Could it be he had really finished with Maureen, seen through her at last. It seemed too good to be true, but she could hope.

She drank her cold coffee. She'd go

down to the cottage right away, tidy up, buy in some food. New enthusiasm filled her. Perhaps everything now was going to start going right. It was almost as if Geoff had been some kind of catalyst, telling her how lucky she was had been a good luck talisman. She smiled to herself. Somehow she thought he would like to have been called that.

She hummed to herself as she drove across the moor. There were lambs, foals, the promise of spring everywhere. A new beginning.

Kaye had put a bowl of blue hyacinths on the office desk, their perfume filled the room with sweetness.

She was delighted to hear Hugh was returning. As Helen told her the news she looked as if she were about to say something and then changed her mind. Helen guessed it had been to do with Maureen. She was as curious probably as she was herself.

She started to go through the papers on her desk, some of the files Kaye had put there when Geoff had called. She dictated some letters, including one to him thanking him for such a delightful evening, telling him Hugh was returning and she hoped to be able to let him know in a few days about the idea for Christmas. She did not mention the question of a merger or takeover. She felt sure now that with the full order book which Hugh had they would have all the work they could cope with, it would put them back on their feet again.

It was as she signed the last letter that suddenly it was as if someone had stuck a knife in her ribs, the pain seared through her, making her cry out.

Kaye came running from the office.

'Mrs Kendall . . . what on earth . . . ?'

Helen was slumped over the desk, the bottle of pills spilling from her hand, the glass of water knocked to the floor. Her face was ghastly, her lips blue. She gasped out . . . 'Ring Gerry . . . quickly . . . please . . . ' Even through the intensity of the pain she prayed — please don't let anything happen to me now — not when Hugh is coming . . .

As luck would have it Gerry was in the neighbourhood and his receptionist got him on his car radio. He came dashing up the stairs and into the office, taking one look at Helen, he rang for an ambulance. She was scarcely conscious now as he gave her an injection.

'Don't try to talk old girl. You're going to need every ounce of strength. You'll be okay . . . I'm getting you into Mount Green Hospital. Don't worry. Just relax.'

As he spoke the waves of pain became a little less intense, it was difficult to breathe . . . then it was as if she was whirling down, down down into a black blessed nothingness.

She opened her eyes. The light hurt them. Quickly she closed them again. Her mouth felt dry, her tongue stuck to the roof of her mouth. There was a dull ache in her chest, not exactly a pain . . . someone said softly,

'She's coming round, fetch Dr Samson would you nurse.'

Once again her lids fluttered. Some-one was bending over her, she felt them rather than saw them. It was difficult to focus . . . they were dressed in white and there was an odd, sharp smell, not unpleasant, she couldn't quite place it. At last a face swam into sight and the voice said,

'That's it, Mrs Kendall. Everything's fine just lie still.'

'A drink . . . some water please,' she murmured, her lips felt dry, cracked.

'Just a drop.' A firm arm lifted her gently and a few drops of blessed cold water dribbled through her lips. It was an effort to swallow. She sank back against the pillows as a man's voice said,

'How are you feeling, Mrs Kendall?' She opened her eyes again. A tall dark man in a white coat stood looking down at her, smiling.

She tried to give an answering smile, 'Nothing really, I mean I don't feel anything, at least I don't think I do. What on earth has been going on?' He picked up her hand, his fingers feeling for her pulse.

'You had a heart attack.' He pretended to look sternly at her now, 'which I am sure will come as no surprise to you from what your own doctor told me,' he said drily. 'We shan't be giving you the award of the year for being sensible over your health I am afraid.'

'No I suppose I deserved that comment . . . so what is the position now?'

'We had to operate, but I am glad to say it was pretty straightforward, no complications. It is now just a matter of rest and doing what you are told.' His eyes twinkled now, belying his tone, 'I get the impression that is something you are not particularly good at.'

Helen swallowed the lump in her throat. 'Do you mean . . . am I . . . shall I . . . ?'

'No' he smiled again, 'Don't worry.

Everything will be okay if you behave yourself. In a few months you will be able to lead a normal life, but when I say normal I mean being sensible and not trying to ask too much of the wonderful machinery of the human body. You drove yours to the edge, but I think we have managed to do what I might call the maintenance job necessary!'

'I suppose I did really ask for it,' she said slowly.

He took the chart from the hook at the end of the bed and ran his finger down it, then he said slowly, 'It should have been done months ago, you know that from your own doctor, and your husband tells me he knew nothing of your condition.'

Helen's eyes flew wide open, 'Hugh's here?'

The doctor nodded. 'Yes, he arrived when you were actually on the operating table. I'm afraid it was a bit of a shock, but fortunately we could tell him by then that you were going to be all right.'

'Oh my God, poor Hugh. Can I see him?'

'Of course, as long as you promise not to get too excited.'

And suddenly he was there — thinner, neatly dressed, tanned, somehow looking younger although his brow was furrowed with anxiety. He bent and kissed her, holding her to him for a moment gently, tentatively as though she were a piece of fragile china.

'Oh Hugh, I shan't snap in two,' she grinned, the tears behind her lids as she remembered how he used to be just the same when Gail was a baby, terrified in case he should drop her or harm her in some way. All tenderness . . .

'Darling, you gave me such a fright. It was a terrible shock and then when Gerry told me how you'd been ill for so long and never said a word . . . why on earth didn't you tell me?'

He glanced away for a moment, squeezing her hand, 'You know you're all that really matters; the business, everything else is nothing. You've no idea how I missed you in Oz . . . and then when I came home to this it was as if the world had ended. Then they wouldn't let me see you for hours . . . are you sure you're okay?'

She nodded, 'Yes, a bit sore, rather tired, I don't actually know what exactly they've done,' she hesitated a moment, 'but I'm happy now you're here, now you're back.'

He kissed her once more, then he got up and walked across to the window, looking out at the flower beds bright with spring flowers, wallflowers, daffodils nodding in the March breeze.

Then he began to talk softly. 'I don't know how to say this. It's silly but words are so inadquate. I realise I've made a complete idiot of myself. I don't even dare to think how you really feel about me now. I can only beg you to forgive me. It was some kind of madness, a drug if you like.'

Helen could tell what difficulty he was having telling her this. She longed to help but knew she had to leave it to him to tell it in his own way.

'Somehow we had got out of tune. I suppose it happens in a lot of marriages, particularly perhaps for people who work together in the same business . . . a kind of staleness enters into the relationship. It needs something to jolt you into realising how lucky you are. In a way Maureen did just that when I found out what she was really like. It was obvious directly we reached Oz. As soon as something, someone turned up who was different . . . she was popular at once out there, spoke the same language. She had a fresh date every night. I know she despised me for what I was, for the very fact that I had allowed myself to become infatuated with her, which is all it was I realise now. It sounds odd, but that is the truth. Anyway she's married a tycoon, someone in the textile business out there, a German with factories all over the place, he's in the film business as well, she did some modelling, had a test, that's how they met.'

He turned back now and drew out

the chair at the side of the bed, sitting down and taking her hand in both his.

'Promise me you're going to be okay, Darling? I've tried to get all the truth I can out of the medics, but you know how cagey they are.'

She nodded, 'Yes I know, but when Gerry first told me about this trouble, when I had the first pains, about the time of Gail's wedding, he did tell me if I had an operation they could put the trouble right. It's something I was born with, some defect to do with the arteries I think he said. I don't really understand — don't know that I want to so long as I never have that awful pain again.' She grimaced, 'It was a lot worse than having Gail I can tell you!'

'My poor darling,' He kissed the palm of her hand. 'Would you like us to sell the business, get right away? I'll get a job of some kind, perhaps we could live abroad, even in Oz.'

It sounded inviting. For a moment she was tempted . . . then she remembered Geoff, the thrill she had felt at the idea of designing again, of the years she and Hugh had spent building up the business, and now of Powdermills. She shook her head.

'Not unless you really want to. With your full order book and some news I've got as well, we'll carry on. And I really would be sorry to leave Powdermills.'

'That's an idea! Why don't we sell the cottage and build on up there? Make a new start in every way?'

Before Helen had time to answer the nurse came bustling in. 'Time for you to go now, Mr Kendall. Your wife needs all the rest she can get.'

He got to his feet, 'Of course. I'll be back in the morning if that's okay.'

The girl nodded, 'Yes, and by the way there was a message and some flowers from a Mr Tasker.'

'Oh poor Michael. He must have wondered what on earth had happened to me,' she said quickly, feeling guilty that the meeting with Geoff had somehow pushed him to the back of her mind. 'How kind of him, could you give him a ring please Hugh?'

He smiled at her, 'I'll do better than that, I'll go and see him, make sure everything's okay up there. After all if it's going to be our home I'll need to spend some time looking round.'

Once more he bent and kissed her. 'Funny how spring comes around every year with new hope, new life. We forget sometimes it isn't only nature that has to remember that!' He grinned at the nurse, 'What was it the poet said . . . 'If winter comes can spring be far behind . . . ' fancy me remembering that from my long ago schooldays.'

At the door he turned and blew a kiss to Helen. She put out her hand, pretending to catch it and hold it tight. A silly, childish little habit they had when they were first in love. A kind of secret sign they had as all lovers do when they are first in love.

Now a great weariness crept over Helen, but it was a contented weariness. She closed her eyes, a little smile hovered round her lips. Spring wasn't far behind, in fact it was here. She could smell the sweet perfume of it and outside the window a thrush was pouring out a great rush of liquid song into the March sunshine. 'It's going to be all right,' she said softly, 'everything is going to be for the best in the best of all possible worlds. Why did I ever doubt it?'

THE END